FLORILLA

A Pinelands Romance

FLORILLA
A Pinelands Romance

A novel by
Perdita Buchan

Plexus Publishing, Inc.
Medford, New Jersey

First printing, 2021

Florilla: A Pinelands Romance

Copyright © 2021 by Perdita Buchan

Published by:
Plexus Publishing Inc.
143 Old Marlton Pike
Medford, NJ 08055
www.plexuspublishing.com

Library of Congress Cataloging-in-Publication Data
Names: Buchan, Perdita, 1940- author.
Title: Florilla : a Pinelands romance / a novel by Perdita Buchan.
Description: Medford, New Jersey : Plexus Publishing, Inc., [2021] |
    Series: A Pinelands romance
Identifiers: LCCN 2021030982 | ISBN 9781940091099 (hardcover) | ISBN
    9781940091082 (paperback) | ISBN 9781940091914 (epub)
Classification: LCC PS3552.U315 F56 2021 | DDC 813/.54--dc23
LC record available at https://lccn.loc.gov/2021030982

Hardcover ISBN 978-1-940091-09-9
Softcover ISBN 978-1-940091-08-2

Printed and bound in the United States of America.

President and CEO: Thomas H. Hogan, Sr.
Graphics and Production: Tiffany Chamenko
Cover Design: Erica Pannella
Sales and Administrative Support: Deb Kranz
Marketing and Publicity: Rob Colding

Composition and typesetting by Jacqueline Crawford.

www.plexuspublishing.com

Dedication

For Cressida

Benderville, The Pines

1848

1

At the first clash of the cupola bell, a cloud of birds rose from the pines into the pale April sky. Benjamin Bender glanced at his gold watch, then at the birds, remarking towhees, cedar waxwings, yellow warblers, the harbingers of spring. From the neat picket gate, he looked with satisfaction down Main Street, a brilliant strip of white sand still bearing the marks of last night's raking.

Gable end to the street, the Benderville Mill rose high above the surrounding forest. In front of it, a stone bridge crossed the millrace, carrying Main Street toward the bell tower and the mill. From the cottages to the south, a stream of people rose and grew, flowed down the road, over the bridge and through the doors to the mill where two men stood marking names in a ledger book. Their progress was well ordered, and if they laughed or talked or sang, the sounds were drowned by the tolling. The two overseers followed them inside, closing the doors as the last notes of the bell died in a faint trembling of the air.

Benjamin Bender looked down at his watch. The birds resettled, only to rise again when the noise of the looms began. As the sound gained a steady rhythm, the circling birds returned and Benjamin Bender looked expectantly up Main Street to the north, toward the forge, the grist mills, and the stables.

The sight that met his eyes, however, was not the expected one: his own wagons bringing raw cotton from the river landing some miles distant. What approached instead was the caricature of a wagon, built out of the spare parts of half a dozen discarded wrecks, driven by a gray-haired Black man and drawn by an old white mule.

"Bless my soul," Benjamin Bender said, "Dr. Peace."

Dr. Peace came to Benderville from time to time when someone was ill or wanted his advice. The old man lived nowhere; he traveled endless miles through the Pines, carrying his doctoring from hamlet to isolated farm. So many were the doctor's stops that the white mule, Bet, stopped dead when she reached any kind of building. He was often seen, a bent, determined figure, hauling and coaxing to get her past a ruin where no one had lived for years. He was not a qualified doctor. Born of two freed slaves, he had little formal schooling. Many of his cures had been learned from the local Indians and the study of whatever medical and botanical books came his way, many of these provided by Benjamin Bender himself.

As the wagon drew nearer at Bet's solemn pace, Benjamin Bender saw that Dr. Peace had a passenger, a girl of eleven or so.

"Here we are then, Bet," Dr. Peace said to the mule, who, at the sight of so many buildings had come to an abrupt halt. The child beside him looked around with wonder but without fear.

"Move up to the fence, man," Benjamin Bender called. "My cotton wagons are coming."

The child jumped down, and, after some cajoling, got Bet to move forward. Stiffly, Dr. Peace climbed down.

Just then, the first of the cotton wagons appeared out of the trees, the trotting mules groomed to a black gloss, harness bright with brass, on the wagons in gold lettering: BENDERVILLE MILL, BENDERVILLE, NEW JERSEY.

Benjamin Bender frowned at his watch. The morning was out of kilter. The wagons were ten minutes late.

"This," said Dr. Peace of the child, "is Florilla Munion."

"Ah, is it?" said Benjamin Bender, shifting uncomfortably under the child's steady gaze.

"Well," he said to the doctor, "did you come for a purpose? I have had no reports of illness."

"No. No illness. I wanted to talk to you. Florilla will stay in the garden."

Obediently, the child held back as the two men walked up the steps across the veranda and into the big house.

Florilla had been in the garden many times before. In the five years she had lived with her grandmother, she had roamed most of the Pines. Old Peggy Munion had lived alone so long she was barely aware of the child's existence. The trees were more real to her, and she talked to them more often.

On hot summer nights, when the air in the shack was thick and stale and full of the dark shapes of her grandmother's troubled dreams, Florilla would slip outside. Sometimes the night was hazy, but sometimes the moonlight was so bright on the creeks and marshes that she felt she was swimming in light.

On one such night, she had found the unexpected world of Benderville, a mysterious town in the wilderness: huge buildings at whose purpose she could only guess, neat rows of clapboard cottages, and, at the center of it all, a house like a castle, surrounded by a garden filled with trees and plants she could not name.

Many times, a light had burned in the long windows of one of the downstairs rooms, and she had seen Benjamin Bender at his desk. Once she had had to hide in the hydrangeas because he had flung the French windows open and stepped onto the veranda to stand for a long time with his hands clasped behind his back.

At other times, a Black woman had come gliding from the kitchen into the woods carrying a bundle of clothes and a wicker basket. Several times, Florilla had followed her bobbing lantern. The woman waited among the night shadows until she heard the faint sounds of hooves and the creak of a wagon. Although the drivers changed, the wagon was always the same, an ordinary farm wagon filled with hay. The woman would give a low call, like one of the night birds. At once, people would struggle up from under the hay in the wagon bed, Black people, men, women, children, sometimes babies. Silent, even the babies, they took the bundles of clothes and the food from the wicker basket. Then they would disappear beneath the hay. The wagon would move on and the woman would slip back into the trees. Obviously, the people in the wagon were on a long and perilous journey, but who were they?

Now here she was in the garden in daylight; the house was no longer a moonlit castle but a rambling stucco building with Gothic eaves and a veranda running around it. Across the road, the biggest building, silent at night, rang with unfamiliar sound.

In the study, Dr. Peace explained things to Benjamin Bender. The child was Florilla Munion, the granddaughter of old Peggy Munion, known to most of the Pinelands as a witch. In reality, she was merely old and cunning, her ways eccentric. It was her lonely position—unwed, unrelated, living in a shack deep in the woods near Sim Place—that made others fear her. The Pines, after all, were a desolate place: acres and acres of pitch pine and blackjack oak, broken only by marsh and river. Her son, Florilla's father, Jack Munion, who called himself The Wizard of the Pines, was a magician. But that was just a trade like being a fiddler or a sign painter.

"Munion left her with her grandmother five years ago," Dr. Peace said. "I came by yesterday and found the old woman dead. We buried her in the clearing. And I have brought the child to you."

"But she has a father. The magician."

"There's more to tell," Dr. Peace said. "Maybe because she's run wild most of her life—I don't know—Peggy Munion told me she had powers."

"Powers?"

Benjamin Bender was curious. Although he considered himself a thoroughly rational man, and the building of an industrial community in the heart of the wilderness a supremely rational plan, he was also keenly interested in forces that were beyond any such control. He saw no contradiction in this. He was a man of his time and once had been impressed by a demonstration of table rapping by the Fox sisters.

"She can heal," Dr. Peace said. "I've seen her do it. She did it with Peggy Munion, with her pain. She did it with hurt animals she found. She knows things the way an animal does. She was waiting for me on the road yesterday. She knew I was coming."

"Yes, yes," said Benjamin Bender. None of this seemed spectacular.

"If Jack Munion knows what he's got, what sort of life will that give her?"

"The family trade, I suppose."

Benjamin Bender glanced at the French windows. He hoped the child wasn't trampling on the beds or picking things.

"Ain't it what you believe though?" Dr. Peace said.

"What? Isn't *what* what I believe?"

Dr. Peace smiled, remembering all the evenings when he had sat at table with Benjamin Bender and listened to his social theories. He knew the story of Benderville by heart. Benjamin Bender had chosen this tract of land in the Pines almost equidistant from New York and Philadelphia, with plentiful waterpower and a poor population, to set up a profitable cotton mill that would provide a reasonable life for anyone willing to work. Housing was provided, cottages for married workers and boarding houses for unmarried men and women. Each child was to be educated to a certain level, and even those who worked as bobbin doffers in the mill had their schedules adjusted to permit this.

"Education," Dr. Peace said.

"Has she had no education?"

"Traveling," Dr. Peace said. "She and her mother traveled with Munion until her mother got sick. Then he left the two of them in the cottage in Sea Grove."

"Cottage in Sea Grove?"

Dr. Peace stared past him as if at the open sea.

"Belonged to her mother's family. Nobody there but one old servant. Nobody else when her mother died. And nobody at all when old Peggy Munion went. You've had orphans in the town here, Mr. Bender. You've let them stay."

"They were fostered by other families. And the child's not an orphan. She does have a father."

In the garden, Florilla touched the stamen of a daffodil and made patterns with the yellow dust on the back of her hand. The April garden was not like the garden of summer. Still, its shape intrigued her, the geometric patterns of the still empty beds, the symmetrical skeletons of the trees.

She was curious about the big house. She remembered big houses from early in her childhood, from the towns where her father gave his magic shows. He talked about the life lived in those houses as though it were something fine. Her mother, he said with a rough laugh, had lived in places like that before she met him, to which she gave no answer. But they didn't have a house at all, just the caravan, and sometimes a room in a cheap boarding house. Florilla liked her bed in the wagon, an alcove like a high cupboard with a railing. She liked the sounds of the animals in their cages, the doves and rabbit and the black hen. She didn't like waking in the night to hear her father shouting, her mother sobbing. She had been glad when he left them at Sea Grove.

Sea Grove was barely a town, settled by Quakers who had built a haphazard collection of summer cottages around an open pavilion where the Sunday meetings were held. Jonathan Siddall, Florilla's uncle, still kept a cottage there and was willing to let his sister and the child, his niece, stay there. After all, it was empty save for an old family retainer who lived in the back rooms and could be counted on to look after things. Mrs. Boswell was a tall, thin forbidding woman, not happy to have her solitude invaded by a frail woman and a child.

At first, Florilla had found her room in the cottage peculiar because she slept alone in it, and it didn't move. The view from the window out over dunes and sea never changed. In this stillness, her mother was weak but happier. She taught Florilla to read so she would understand that there was a world beyond the dunes and the cottage and the little town of Sea Grove that closed its gates to the outside world on Sundays.

One Sunday, Jack Munion had come in the wagon, and when they turned him back, he released a flock of crows, a number of which came to roost in the rafters of the pavilion cawing raucously.

After that, Mrs. Boswell, who remembered Florilla's mother as a child, became kinder. When Sarah Siddall died, and Munion came to take Florilla, she protested. But hers was the only dissenting voice. Jonathan Siddall was in Europe, and to the rest of the family, Sarah Siddall was already dead, disowned when she ran off with the wizard.

So Florilla had made the journey by caravan deep into the Pines. She missed her mother, but at first the doves and the rabbit and the hen made up for it. Then, when Munion left on his travels, they were gone too.

"All right," Benjamin Bender said, at last, persuaded by the possibility of an educational experiment, "you can leave her here. She will have to go

to school and do some work in the mill like the other children her age.
She can live here for the moment. Bring her in so that I may talk to her."

Florilla had never been in a library. She stared at the rows of books,
their polished spines like candy: black licorice, amber horehound,
crimson cherry. She wanted to touch them, but instead looked down at
the Oriental carpet, patterned like the garden. She could almost feel the
warm colors through her bare feet. Dr. Peace sat hunched in his chair,
just the way he drove the wagon. Benjamin Bender sat behind his desk.

"Well, Florilla," he said, "your friend Dr. Peace has persuaded me
that you should come to live at Benderville."

Florilla looked at Dr. Peace, who nodded his head. She didn't know
what living at Benderville would mean, but she knew that she didn't
want to go back to her grandmother's shack at Sim Place or to travel
with her father. She was curious about the books and the houses and
the mill Dr. Peace had told her about.

"Yes," she said.

"You must understand," he went on, "that this is a working community, and you must be part of it."

Florilla tried to read the gold lettering on the spines of the books but
some were letters that she did not recognize: triangles and backward p's.

"You will go to school in the mornings and work several afternoons
in the mill as a bobbin doffer for your keep."

Florilla didn't understand his words any more than she understood
the words on the spines of the books, but he was smiling at her, and so
she smiled back.

Benjamin Bender wondered if she were a little simple.

"Very well," he said, "it is time for my rounds, so I will show you
Benderville."

Everything was extraordinary to Florilla: the horse barn, the mule barn, the carriage barn, all spotless, every piece of harness polished and in its place. The mules were used for daily work, carrying the finished cloth south to the landing on the Wading River and bringing the raw cotton shipments back. The horses, standing in deep straw, their coats still winter rough, were used for occasions: weddings, funerals, Benjamin Bender's trips to the river landing or the nearby port of Tuckerton. In the carriage barn were ordinary wagons, two phaetons, a potbellied pumper painted bright red, winking with brass, gold-lettered BEND-ERVILLE FIRE COMPANY NO. 1. Benjamin Bender walked round it, laying a hand on its metal belly. It rang faintly where he patted it.

"Fires, I needn't tell you, are the greatest danger in the Pines."

They passed by the forge, gristmill, and sawmill, while the sounds of the looms grew as they drew nearer to the main mill building. The ground vibrated perceptibly under their feet, and Florilla felt herself begin to tremble with it.

"Now you see," said Benjamin Bender, raising his voice to compensate, "the cotton mill provides the livelihood of the town. The hours for workers are six a.m. to six p.m., and the pay is a dollar twenty-five a day. All workers are provided with housing, garden, seed if wanted, the use of company carriages on the occasions of weddings and funerals. The properties must be well maintained. Neatness means attention to your surroundings. That sort of attention is very necessary to work in the mills. Attention to one's work must be constant, or the result is an uneven weave. Also the machinery itself is extremely dangerous. It can kill you for inattention."

Florilla was too frightened to ask how. She had only a confused image of some sort of furious monster, and she was trembling by the time they reached the double doors of the mill itself. Above the door, on a heavy stone lintel, were carved strange words that Florilla didn't recognize.

"That," said Benjamin Bender, "is an inscription in the Latin tongue, something you may learn if you show aptitude for your studies. It is translated "We Labor as a Family." I like to think of Benderville as a true family."

"Perhaps," he added, smiling faintly, "because I myself have no children."

Florilla scarcely heeded his words. She was staring up at the even rows of windows. She saw that many were filled with the green leaves of plants, in some cases framing the faces of children, like angels looking down from some celestial garden.

Benjamin Bender pulled open the door. Inside, a spiral staircase wound upwards, climbing into a roaring like waves in a storm. They passed the carding floor, the spinning floor, climbing to the weaving floor where the noise was a physical assault. Florilla was never sure what to her was the greatest horror of that moment, the violent clash and clatter of the machines or the sight, down that long bare room, of row after row of looms all thundering and shaking like some evil captive energy, waiting only to break from its moorings and slay its captors, those intent watchful women and girls. Occasionally, a child would jump down from its seat on the windowsill and dart among the looms. "Bobbin doffers." The words came back into her mind. Light poured through the many windows, striking bright metal, mocking the way it shone on dew or water.

Benjamin Bender motioned to one of the men who walked among the looms. They stood together for several minutes, talking, apparently able to hear each other over the din. One of the children running by gave her a curious look. Benjamin Bender did not even notice Florilla's fear. He saw nothing to be afraid of, just a peaceful army doing battle against want and idleness.

Afterward, they walked down the main street past the two boarding houses for unmarried male and female workers and on past the cottages of the married workers. Each, as Benjamin Bender pointed out, with ample space for a garden that could be planted with vegetables and fruit trees.

Florilla was handed into the charge of Ananda and Lethe, Benjamin Bender's two Black servants. Tall, silent Lethe was Ananda's daughter. It was she Florilla had seen on her nighttime travels. Ananda grumbled kindly, but Lethe simply moved in and out of the shadows of the big back kitchen as Florilla had seen her move silently in and out of the shadows of the woods.

Ananda showed Florilla to the room at the top of the back stairs that was to be hers, small and simply furnished, with a patched quilt on the wooden bed and a view out over the garden.

"You can put your things in this chest," Ananda said, but Florilla had no things. So Ananda took her by the hand, led her downstairs, out the door, and down the road to the company store for lengths of Benderville cotton to make her dresses.

At six o'clock, Benjamin Bender stood at the gate for the ringing out. It was dusk; in winter it had been dark. At the first stroke of the bell, the doors swung open, and the morning's army marched out again. Some of them moved wearily, and perhaps they didn't talk or laugh or sing. But against the reverberations of the bell, it was impossible to hear.

2

For the first few days, Florilla was left to her own devices. Benjamin Bender believed that if she did not stay at Benderville of her own free will, she would not stay at all. She must learn to love the place. The premise of Benderville was that its citizens should love it and the mill that supported it.

The noise and movement of Benderville was strange to Florilla. At Sim Place there had been only silence save for the sounds of the woods, of wind and rain. Her grandmother's mutterings had seemed as elemental. There had been no more routine in the days than there was in the weather, only the cycle of the seasons. Before that, her memories of Sea Grove had been of a mother who woke her in the night to watch the full moon on the water, who rose sometimes at sunrise, sometimes at noon, and then did not rise at all.

The Benderville mansion seemed in its own way as full of the props of magic as her father's wagon. She touched the surfaces of bronze and marble and polished wood. Dark shapes of claw-footed furniture rose out of the gloom like mythical animals, while bell jars held familiar woodland creatures, trapped and still. Marble busts of men, set on pillars, watched her with blank eyes. On their heads were wreaths of leaves she recognized as laurel. The only full statue was of a woman, either emerging from or turning into a tree, glancing over her shoulder in terror. Florilla touched the cold silky marble as if to comfort her.

The house with its stairs and corridors was its own landscape. At night, she wandered through it on bare, silent feet. Sometimes she stood outside Benjamin Bender's door listening to his breathing. Sometimes he woke and lit the lamp, and then she would flee down the hall. Florilla knew she was not always the only one awake in the house. Many nights, Lethe went on her errand in the woods, returning at dawn. Once Lethe was gone, Florilla sometimes stole into Ananda's room and stared down at the stolidly sleeping face. Ananda slept with a kerchief tied round her head, her face as still as a dark pool. Standing by the bed, Florilla could see into her dreams, saw trees hung with Spanish moss, flat fields under a motionless sky, seeds that flew like milkweed from the split boles of an unfamiliar plant. Ananda slept on.

On the third day, a sudden wave of homesickness sent Florilla all the way to Sim Place. She took the familiar track around the open spong, across a wide expanse of marsh grass dotted with leatherleaf bushes showing their first white bells of bloom. Here and there rose the bleached and broken trunks of dead trees. Then the pinewoods closed around her, and she knew it was not far to the clearing. She was dawdling along, drawn, yet in no hurry, when she heard a horse whinny. Florilla stopped in her tracks, heart pounding. She left the path and made her way from tree to tree until she was in sight of the shack. The little building leaned away from her, already looking more ramshackle, more abandoned. In front of it stood a familiar caravan, a gray horse between the shafts, head up, ears forward. The wooden sides of the wagon were painted with birds and flowers in bright colors and among them the words:

J.J. MUNION
MAGICIAN AND FORTUNE TELLER
THE WIZARD OF THE PINES

Florilla shrank back. The horse, aware of her presence, turned its head and whinnied again. This time a man came out of the shack. He was a small man, bandy legged, wearing a felt hat that largely obscured his face. He wore britches and boots, and the sleeves of his smock were rolled up so that the sun glinted on the blond hairs of his forearms. He looked around him, and Florilla wondered in panic if he had a trick that allowed him to see through trees. But, after a moment, he went back inside, and Florilla, faint with terror, slipped back into the woods.

She was halfway across the emptiness of the spong when she heard the sound of the horse's hooves, slurred by the sand of the road. Quickly she darted into a thicket of leatherleaf bushes.

Slowly the wagon came out of the trees. Jack Munion sat on the box, the reins loose on the horse's back. Every so often he would pull the horse up and look around him. Florilla knew he was looking for her. Her grandmother had said he didn't have powers, he just knew tricks.

"The powers," her grandmother said, "come every third generation. That is you, my girl. He knows it. Take care."

She was afraid all the same. He was strong. She remembered him drunk and shouting, shoving her grandmother against the flimsy walls of the shack. Suddenly Benderville, her little room, the gardens, Ananda and Lethe, even the mill seemed like a haven if only she could reach it. The horse snorted as the caravan passed near Florilla's hiding place.

"Something hiding?" Munion said in his flat voice. "Or maybe someone?"

Florilla concentrated on the horse till it dropped its head and tore at the marsh grass. Munion swore, jerked its head up, and the caravan creaked on, disappearing into the woods. It was a long time before Florilla dared to move. But when she did, she ran, cutting in and out of the trees until she reached the path that led to the back gate of the mansion garden. She burst through it, across the back lawn and through the dim recesses of the kitchen.

"Lord, child!" Ananda exclaimed.

Florilla ran on down the hall. Outside the library door she paused to get her breath, then knocked rapidly.

"Come in."

Benjamin Bender looked up to see the disheveled child standing in the doorway.

"Florilla," he said.

"I want to stay," Florilla burst out, "I want to stay here. I'll work in the mill, but I want you to teach me the spells."

"Spells?"

"In the books."

Florilla went to the bookcase and pointed to the books with the triangles and backward p's on the spine. She was sure they must contain a strong magic, that, once learned, could keep her safe.

"These books."

Benjamin Bender laughed.

"Those aren't spells. That is a language called ancient Greek."

"Teach it to me," Florilla said.

"Do you think you could learn it?'

"I know I could."

Benjamin Bender regarded her curiously. There was something unusual about the child.

"Well, well," he said. "We'll see."

And so Florilla began her days at the Benderville School, in the schoolhouse under the catalpa trees. Magreavey the schoolmaster was a nervous young man. He had been hired from Philadelphia and found himself in a wilderness haunted by tales of strange creatures like the Jersey Devil, born at Leeds Point to an exhausted wife who prayed that her thirteenth child would be the devil himself. The baby, with the head of a goat and the tail of a serpent, had flown up the chimney, to maraud forever in the Pines, killing livestock and frightening humans. At night, reading his Bible in his cottage, Magreavey was sure he heard the beating of leathery wings. And now he was being asked to teach some wild creature, the granddaughter of a witch who had lived with her in the woods much of her life. He also found Benjamin Bender's theories of education trying at times. Games were used to teach counting and spelling and vocabulary. Learning should be joyous, the failure to learn its own punishment. This, Magreavey felt, was not always evident to his pupils. Florilla, however, was a revelation. She knew the questions before she was asked. She devoured books. He had no need to make up games and entertainments for her. He spoke to Benjamin Bender about her progress—he could not contain her within the curriculum.

"Well, Magreavey," Benjamin Bender said, "perhaps she could learn Greek and Latin. It's been a long time since I had a pupil."

"I'm certain she could, but is there any point in teaching classics to a girl?"

"A little like teaching a dog to walk on its hind legs, you mean?"

Mr. Magreavey shrugged and smiled.

"Point taken," said Benjamin Bender, "and yet there's really no harm. If you raise one mind, it will touch others. A mind trained is a mind saved."

Benjamin Bender was amazed at how quickly Florilla did learn. He would watch her bent over the books in wonderment that she was not a boy. She should have been. She should have been his son, a proper receptacle, not a ragtag orphan girl with psychic powers and a grandmother the Pinelands considered a witch. There was no sense in it. Yet here she was, copying exercise after exercise, memorizing vocabulary and grammar, reciting precisely, perfectly. She was a marvel.

They worked in the cool of the morning for an hour after the ringing in bell, and again in the evening after the ringing out. Florilla was glad to spend the early mornings in the darkness of the library, the shutters closed against the sun and the raging colors of the garden. She had not yet started in the weave room and so, for the rest of the day, except for the time it took to do her homework, Florilla was free. On the hottest days, she worked in the back scullery, which had a flagstone floor and was very cool. On other days, she would go out into the garden and lie in the shade of the black walnuts.

The mansion's garden was planted with ornamental trees and shrubs that flowered in succession: redbuds, magnolias, lilacs, fruit trees, crepe myrtle. The flowerbeds were brilliant with flowers, only the most ordinary of which—phlox, daisies, hollyhocks—had she seen before. She might have been in another country altogether. Beds of lilies grew in all colors, borders of yarrow, salvia, California poppies, bellflowers. Lupines grew, dianthus, and tall spears of yucca. The place buzzed with insects, throbbed with birdsong.

Florilla loved the hollyhocks with their heavy, velvety heads of pink and cream and deep crimson. She loved, too, the huge blue hydrangea bushes along the veranda. Lethe had bunches of these hanging to dry in the scullery, their petals turning a brittle, ghostly silver.

The garden blazed, pulsed, warred with color. The colors of Sim Place had been greens and browns, the only brilliance the white sand, the only flowers the trillium and the pale yellow orchids growing in the ferny gloom. Sometimes Florilla walked with Benjamin Bender in the garden in the evening. She liked the way dusk washed out the colors of the flowers, making them ghosts of themselves. Then the shapes were clearer, the stiff stalks of the yucca, the lacy phlox, the motionless rain of a willow.

"I can grow anything here," Benjamin Bender said. "As long as there is water enough and good soil brought in, I can grow anything grown on this continent. This garden is my America."

On a stone bench were the words of Cicero:

Si hortum cum bibliotheca habes, nihil deerit.

Florilla translated:

"If you have a garden in a library, nothing will be missing."

"Correct," Benjamin Bender said, "though often translated as 'If you have a garden and a library, you have everything you need,' the actual translation refers to the fact that Roman libraries were often in their gardens."

3

The Fourth of July was a holiday in Benderville, the occasion of a full town outing to a stretch of beach owned by the Benderville Mill. The mill was closed, the machinery shut down, the cotton wagons commandeered to carry the workers with such a shouting and singing that Florilla couldn't help laughing, feeling her spirits lift with the good will of it. Benjamin Bender drove one of the phaetons, Florilla sat beside him, Ananda, Lethe and the schoolmaster packed in the back. Mr. Magreavey would have much preferred a day to himself to read his Bible in the empty town. On these outings, he was expected to lead groups of children on explorations of the natural world, identifying shells and the flowers and grasses of the dunes. The prospect of education through the senses filled him, as usual, with gloom. All the girls of the boarding house rode in one wagon, and in another the young men who jumped down frequently to proffer bunches of dusty roadside flowers to their girls.

The day was hot, and the flies were bad, and the beach five miles distant. Dark streaks of sweat marked the horses' flanks by the time the road came out of the shade of the pines into the flat, glaring expanse of salt marsh. Ahead a bright haze hung in the air. The road swung south, the marsh gave way to sand, and Florilla saw at last the great glittering expanse of water.

On the beach, fires were started for the clambake. Freed from the silencing of the machines, strong voices of men and women rose above the roar of the waves. Mechanics, who worked on the huge gears of the mill machinery, their trousers rolled up to the knees, plunged in and out of the breakers. The children played too, shrieking and splashing, but the women held back. The older women settled themselves in groups, spreading out blankets, admonishing the babies and small children. But it was the young women that Florilla watched, the mill girls. They stood in little groups, laughing and giggling together, their eyes on the exploits of the men. They would go only to the edge of the wet sand and no further. Florilla saw that most of the girls her age, the ones she went to school with and who seldom spoke to her, hung back in their own little group.

At Sea Grove she had explored the beaches in all seasons, had learned to swim, her mother watching from the shore. Suddenly, a quick anger at the girls simpering on the beach made her run from the dunes, stumbling in the soft sand, into the foamy edge of the water, then on, waist deep, her skirts billowing and dragging at her as she struggled to fling herself beyond the first breakers. Far away, she heard the sound of female screaming. She plunged on, throwing herself over the glassy crest of a breaking wave. She had not counted, however, on the weight of her full skirts. They clung to her, trammeled her legs so that she was pulled down, couldn't kick free. The undertow dragged at her, a wave caught her, and she was rolled over again and again till she thought her lungs would burst, slammed into the sand. A hand reached out and caught her, pulling her up.

Florilla blinked the water out of her eyes. The girl holding her hand was Fiona Fitzgerald, daughter of the Benderville paymaster. She was a tall girl with heavy black hair in a braid hanging down her back who sat at the back of the schoolroom. Now she smiled.

"Can you swim?" she said.

"I could if I didn't have all these clothes."

"I can too," Fiona said and smiled again.

After that, they were friends. Fiona hated school, but she loved the woods, which she knew almost as well as Florilla herself. She was not burdened with summer lessons, nor did she yet have to work in the mills. She had five brothers and lived in one of the three bigger houses near the mansion.

"Mother has me always working." She made a face. "Those boys make endless work. The big ones think they're so important, and the little ones just follow me around."

Here she swooped down and stumbled round in circles, calling in a high child's voice:

"Fee! Fee!"

"The thing is, though," she said straightening up, "boys are more fun, or anyway the things boys can do."

Florilla had not thought of the distinction before. Housework had not been demanded of her, nor had the freedom of shore and woods been restricted.

Fiona looked at her sharply.

"I'd think you were lucky," she said, "living in that big house with servants to do everything for you, except that you have to take lessons with the old man. I couldn't stand that."

"I like it," Florilla said.

"Well," said Fiona, matter-of-factly, "you're smart."

In the early afternoon, when chores were finished, Fiona would whistle like a catbird in the trees, and Florilla would leave her books on the veranda and run down the garden. From the kitchen window, Lethe watched, smiling.

Once across the bridge and safe in the cover of the trees, they ran, laughing and pelting each other with ferns torn from the verges. Sunday Lake was Fiona's favorite place. It was really a big pond, fed by one of the finger inlets of the Wading River and screened almost entirely from the surrounding woods and marsh around it by white cedars. There, they shed dresses and petticoats and went skinny dipping. As they stood naked on the bank, Florilla envied Fiona's tawny skin. Her own looked as white as the underbelly of a frog. But under the cedar-colored water, her limbs were almost as dark as Fiona's. The water was warm in the shallows, cold where it flowed in from the river. Sometimes they would race, churning up the placid surface; sometimes they floated lazily through the ragged stripes of sun and shadow.

Beyond the cedars, only a ridge of mossy ground, a tangle of huckleberry and sweet pepper bush screened them from the sand track that led deeper into the woods. In one part of the bank were sundew plants, their sticky leaves breaking the light into droplets. Florilla liked to lie close to them, watching at eye level the struggles of trapped insects.

"If you tied one on your finger," Fiona said, "maybe it would eat away the skin."

Pitcher plants too, grew in the shallows near the bank. They had a cat-like stink in the hot sun. Florilla and Fiona would push each other into them.

Sometimes they would wander deeper into the woods. Once, on the spur of a sand road, they found a collier's clearing. Smelling the bitter wood smoke, they left the path, creeping from tree to tree till they reached a clearing ringed by raw, newly cut stumps. The beehive-shaped pile of wood stood like a primitive burial mound, a thin stream of white steam from the burning charcoal issuing from the top. The collier himself lay sleeping in a three-sided teepee made of cedar poles and turf. Florilla had seen colliers before. Peggy Munion had warned that they were rough and to stay away from them.

"Come on," she said quickly to Fiona. "The sun's getting weaker. It must be near dinnertime, and you said you had to get dinner for the boys."

Fiona's mother was a woman of imposing bulk, with a wide, still face and dark watchful eyes. Her hair, like Fiona's, was the shining solid black of an animal's coat, not like any human hair that Florilla had ever seen. She said little and moved with surprising ease and swiftness for someone of her size. She seemed to bring a hush with her whenever she entered a room. The noisy roughhousing of Fiona and the boys would cease immediately, as the shadow of a hawk stills the chatter of small birds.

She nodded at Florilla.

"The girl that ran loose in the woods at night," she said. "I've seen you."

Florilla had never been aware that anyone other than Lethe walked the woods at night.

"Poppa's never home," Fiona said. "And he's only a lot of bluster. He may run the store and the company payroll, but Momma runs everything else. She's a full-blooded Indian anyway from over at Brotherton."

"What's Brotherton?"

"It's nothing, but it used to be an Indian reservation. They set it up a hundred years ago. Don't you know anything?"

"Not about Indians."

"Well, they all left and went up to New York, all but a few. Her family stayed. So she's Leni Lenape Indian. She knows everything. She knows how to canoe and how to kill people so they don't make a sound. She taught me to swim and to ride. She can make a horse do anything."

Indian Mary, as Florilla heard Fiona's mother called in the village, sometimes worked as a spare hand in the mill. Once, after she began to work in the weave room in late September, Florilla doffed for her. Doffing for someone meant watching their looms and changing the bobbins when they ran out. Indian Mary worked with a deft intentness, a calm economy of movement, as though she were engaged in an elemental task, something ancient and primitive, quite unrelated to the clattering, anxious machinery. She had no trouble watching three looms, and Florilla had little time to dream, so quickly did the bobbins run out. She had the same effect on the girls working near her that she had on her own family: they worked steadily, without any signing to each other or glances toward the window where the afternoon blazed.

Florilla grew used to the mill. It wearied but did not frighten her anymore, though on hot, humid days, the weave room was almost unbearable. The clatter of the looms would become a thundery rumbling, and she would look to the window, hoping to see in a black sky the advent of a cooling storm. The sky would be a clear blue, but the thunder within the looms would increase. Then, just as she thought her head must burst, she reached a place beyond it, like being washed onto a distant shore. Usually it was a familiar landscape: Sim Place with its patches of orchids, the dunes of Sea Grove. But sometimes the rumbling became the waves of oceans she had never seen rolling onto strange beaches.

Sometimes those beaches were long strips of white sand overhung by palms, backed by jungles filled with the cries of parrots; sometimes they were shingle under a gray sky backed by a neat countryside of farms. Sometimes she found herself in unknown houses, walking through rooms and corridors full of statuary and lined with gilded mirrors. Once she stood in a room made entirely of glass where unknown flowers bloomed.

One evening Dr. Peace came to see a patient in the village. It was dark when he made his way up the steps onto the veranda where Benjamin Bender sat waiting for him.

"I am delighted to see you, Doctor," he said. Come in, come in. Ananda has kept some dinner for you."

"How is the child?"

"Well, well. She'll be happy to see you, I'm sure. But I'd like to ask you more about her history. She has become quite a part of this place."

In the scented darkness, the old doctor's mind wandered. He closed his eyes and saw the sand roads blinding under a noon sun, felt the jarring of the wagon, the burning forehead of a child delirious over near Quaker Bridge.

"You'll stay the night," Benjamin Bender was saying. "Your bedroom is made up. Ananda will get one of the men to see to Bet."

The prospect of a comfortable night brought the doctor back to his surroundings. He followed his host into the house.

⟡ ⟡

"Tuberculosis," Dr. Peace said. "That's what killed her mother. She came from a Philadelphia Quaker family. Took up with Munion down at Sea Grove one summer when he was working the shore towns."

"Charmed by the wizard?"

"The girl was young, brought up strict. And Munion has charm when he wants to use it. Folks believe what they want to believe."

He sighed.

"Don't like to think it, but sometimes I wonder if that's how I cure them."

"I suppose," he went on, "Munion thought he'd married a rich girl and that would soften his days. It didn't work out that way. Her family cut her off. She traveled with him for a time, as part of the act, I guess. Then after she got sick, he took her to Sea Grove and left her there in a cottage that belonged to her brother."

Dr. Peace took a mouthful of blueberry pie.

"Munion came looking for me," he said. "He knew I'd looked after the old woman, buried her too. Wanted to know where the child was. I didn't tell him."

"And if he finds out?"

"Money," Dr. Peace said. "He thinks he can use her in his act to make money."

Seeing Dr. Peace in the morning brought Florilla mixed memories. She remembered his kindness and the way he had soothed her grandmother, taught her to make snakeroot tea for the old woman's ailments. She remembered the relief she felt when she saw the white mule coming down the sand road after her grandmother died. But she also remembered the burial in the clearing, the rough grave whose sandy sides kept caving in. She shuddered.

"I'm glad to see you still here," Dr. Peace said. "Mr. Bender tells me you do well in your studies."

Florilla nodded.

He smiled at her. The years of moments snatched for study pressed on him, moments stolen from charcoaling, farming, picking. This child was offered everything, and yet it was not her right and could be snatched from her at any moment. He was Black; she was female. He laid a hand on her head.

"Make the most of it, child," he said. "Do not fail in your opportunities."

Florilla did not understand what he meant. She knew she couldn't fail in her studies, and how could this miraculous world she had found fail her? She looked up into the kind, melancholy face.

"Will my father come for me?" she asked.

"I don't know. Mr. Bender wants to keep you here. He is a powerful man. Don't fret."

For Florilla's lower lip had begun to tremble. The coming of the doctor had brought the past too close. She saw her father, drunk in the shanty, shouting, shoving her grandmother against the wall so that the whole flimsy place shuddered. She shook her head violently to blur the memory.

"I won't," she said defiantly. "I won't go."

"Don't fret, child," the doctor said. "Don't look for things that may not happen."

4

In time, the stories reached Jack Munion's ears, stories of the witch's granddaughter living in splendor at Benderville mansion. He heard it in a tavern in Tuckerton, one of the Benderville workers talking on his day off. If he'd noticed the painted wagon among the several outside, it meant nothing to him.

A day later, Jack Munion drove his wagon down the main street of Benderville, stopped in front of the mansion, and threw the horse's reins over the picket fence. He sauntered through the gate, leaving it ajar behind him, and walked up the veranda steps to rap harshly on the front door. It was answered by Lethe.

"You the knife grinder?" she said.

Jack Munion, who had taken off his hat before knocking, twirled it on his finger, flipped it into the air, and caused it to disappear up his loose sleeve.

"No ma'am," he said, "I'm the wizard."

"Well," said Lethe, "I guess you want the back door."

Jack Munion smiled.

"I want to see Mr. Bender. He seems to have kidnapped my daughter, Florilla."

"You wait here," Lethe said and shut the door.

Munion waited, but he glanced around quickly before retrieving his hat from his sleeve. He waited ten minutes, had raised his hand to knock again, when the door was opened.

"You can come in," Lethe said.

He stepped into the cool gloom of the hall and followed the beacon of Lethe's retreating white pinafore.

"In here," Lethe said, throwing open the door to the library.

Benjamin Bender stood with his back to the window. Jack Munion, hands in pockets, swaggered in, unintimidated. He had done his act in enough town halls and lyceums. This room, with its walls of books, baize-covered desk, and marble mantel looked much the same. Nor was the old man standing there much different from the rich holiday-makers from New York or Philadelphia who secretly hoped to call up spirits for advice and assurance. Men of power and money had the same weaknesses as their gullible workers.

"Well, Mr. Munion," Benjamin Bender said, "what can I do for you?"

"Well, sir," Jack Munion said, "I believe you have my daughter. That's what I heard anyway. In my travels."

He looked down, twisting his hat in his hands.

"I've been looking for her, sir. Up and down. All over these blasted woods. I'm all she has now. Her mother, rest her soul, died young, and her old grandmother, my mother, died while I was gone trying to make a living for us all. When I came back, I found her buried and the child gone. I appreciate what you done for her, taking her in, but I'd like to take her back."

"Her grandmother died in early April," Benjamin Bender said. "It is now October. It has taken you that long to find her a few miles from Sim Place?"

"Well, you didn't leave me any messages when you took her, did you? Could be you told people *not* to tell me. From one end of the Pines to the other, not one soul knows a thing about it. Not even that Black Jim doctor who buried my mother."

He smiled again.

"The child needed a livelihood, Mr. Munion. She came to the one place in the Pines where she could find it, the one community based on education and honest toil, a chance for self-improvement. Would you rather she had gone about the woods knocking huckleberries into a basket?"

"I would rather she came with me, her father, her own flesh and blood. What this place is based on, Mr. Bender, is money. You make money off this mill and the fools who slave in it. You wouldn't bother with a girl like Florilla if you didn't stand to get something out of it. She's got talents, Mr. Bender. She's third generation. It's them that have powers."

Munion stepped nearer.

"She'll have the second sight. She's a healer, a natural for the trade. Maybe she can predict business things too. Or have you got other uses for her right here?"

Benjamin Bender took a deep breath.

"She works as a bobbin doffer in the mill."

"I ain't talking about that. Not what she does in the mill. I mean what she's doing in this house. She's going on twelve, Mr. Bender. She's pretty, like her mother was."

"That's preposterous."

Jack Munion shrugged.

"Most folks wouldn't think so. They find things like that easy to believe. Watch."

He pulled from the pocket of his trousers a bright silk handkerchief. He kept pulling, releasing a rope of multicolored handkerchiefs.

"They're real. Feel them."

He held them out.

"I'm not interested in your tricks, Munion," Benjamin Bender said.

"Well now look," said the wizard. He stuffed the scarves into his two fists, then opened them on nothing. He smiled.

"Gone, ain't they? You believed that, didn't you?"

There was a knock at the door and then it opened, and on the threshold stood Florilla. She looked in horror from her father to Benjamin Bender and ran.

"Florilla!" Munion shouted. "You get right back here."

The front door slammed, but he was after her, down the steps and into the garden in time to see his lost daughter disappear over the footbridge and into the woods.

Munion swore under his breath.

"Devil take the little bitch."

When he turned, the old man was standing on the veranda. He looked all puffed up like a pigeon.

"It seems that she doesn't want to go with you, Munion," he said.

"She's a child," Munion snarled. "What does she know? And how do I know what you been telling her about me?"

"I think you should go. For the present, she is better off here. She has a brilliant mind. Would you deny her the chance for an education?"

"She has talents, Mr. Bender. And you know it. Those are inherited family talents. Would you deny me a livelihood? And her too? What good is an educated woman to the world? About as good as fish that can sing opera. That won't do the fish no good, but it'll make money for the man who owns it. Now, who owns the trained fish? Me or you?"

"No one owns her, man. No one owns another person."

"You don't own them?"

He flung his arm in a broad gesture toward the mill.

"They are not slaves. They are free to go."

"Free," Jack Munion said. "Oh, they're free to go back to the cranberry bogs and get the rheumatics standing thigh deep in water for the picking. They're free to go back to farms so poor you can't raise a weed on 'em, or south to the cotton fields. They're free all right."

"They can choose," Benjamin Bender said calmly. "You chose your life, Mr. Munion, and it cost you your child. I've listened to you long enough. Leave my property or I'll have you thrown off."

"All right," Jack Munion said. "If that's the way you want it. The next time I'll come with a constable. The law knows I'm right. I'm due the labor of my child. I'm owed money. You understand that, Mr. Bender."

"How much money will the loss of her services cost you?"

Munion cast down his eyes.

"I can't put a price on them, not those talents."

Benjamin Bender, reaching into his breast pocket, pulled out a ten-dollar bill. He held it out.

"Would this keep you for a while?

Jack Munion shrugged.

"It won't mend a grieving father's heart," he said sorrowfully. "But if you want to keep her here longer, I'll stay away for a while. But it only buys me off for a while, you know."

He took the bill.

"Get out, Munion."

The wizard picked a sprig of autumn clematis, stuck it in one ear and pulled it out of the other. He dropped the felt hat on his head, went through the gate, and, climbing into the wagon, turned the horse away from the mansion toward the road out of Benderville.

"Good afternoon, Mr. Bender," he called, raising his hat to reveal a white dove and giving a rough shout of laughter.

Jack Munion drove on, whistling. He hadn't got what he'd come for, but there was time for that. Meanwhile, the old fool had made him significantly richer.

5

Autumn deepened. The maples along Benderville's Main Street burned red against the dull brown of the oaks, the solid greens of the pines. In the woods, the sassafras trees turned a blotchy yellow orange, and the sunny places bloomed with asters and goldenrod. The mansion garden lingered on, banked with smoldering coppery chrysanthemums.

On October mornings, Benjamin Bender would come to the gate, gold watch in hand, and stand under the scarlet trees, smelling the salty tang of autumn in the air. As the mill bell began to ring, ducks would rise from the millrace, wings beating the water, and Benjamin Bender would imagine himself back in the New England of his youth. That was the reason he had planted the maples. He thought of Franklinville, Massachusetts, set narrowly in the steep cleft cut by the Blackstar River. He thought of the Blackstar Mills, built just above the river at the foot of the gorge, the red and yellow maples on Indian Top.

He thought of it all, the boarding houses for the Yankee farm girls, the hovels of the immigrant Irish hired for the meanest jobs, children working in the mills at eight years old, families crammed into single rooms with no access to the natural world. Disparate warring elements, not a harmonious community like the one he had founded here in these temperate woodlands. It was on such ideological matters that he had quarreled with his brother Isaiah, who still ran the Blackstar Mills. Of course, those mills turned out gingham of a rare beauty, soft plaids in the colors of the Scottish hills. Here, the product was cruder, but the pattern of human lives woven into it was less bitter, far less bitter.

Winter in the Pines did not have the harsh drama of a New England winter. The woods were scoured at times with a cold northeast wind that eddied the sand of the roads, drenched often with heavy cold rain but little snow. Occasionally, a coastal storm would spend itself over the Pines, snow hissing in the millrace and drifting up against the trees and fences of Main Street. If the snow were very heavy, the mill would shut down while the men shoveled the bridges and paths, packed down the snow on Main Street with the horse-drawn roller. The snow was usually gone in a day or two, eaten away by the salt air until only a few tattered drifts were left. Often, it was cold enough that the sand ruts froze, and the thin clear ice on shallow bog pools shattered like glass. On winter nights, Florilla could see from her bedroom window the fires the colliers built to keep warm, like beacons in the woods. She thought of them when the Christmas tree stood in the parlor before the windows, the candles on its branches reflected in the black panes, murmurs of wonder rising as the entire town of Benderville crowded in.

Mr. Magreavey led the school children in the carol singing while old Tom Cranmer played the fiddle and told tales. He had known Benderville from the time it was called Collinstown and had only a sawmill owned by the two Collins brothers. He remembered their brief flirtation with the silk industry, the clearing of pines for the planting of mulberries which had left a few survivors at the edge of the woods. Now it was all about cotton.

The bleak days of late winter, of cold rain and gray skies, rounded out the year. There was little then to lure anyone beyond the confines of the town. The weave room was like being below decks on a ship plowing its way through a gray sea. Sometimes the rain from the coast foamed against the windows like spume.

And so the seasons turned in Benderville, and through them all thrummed the steady rhythm of the mill. It was the heartbeat of the town, and the time it kept had nothing to do with seasons in the natural world or years in the world of men.

Benderville was so self-contained that few things interrupted its daily pace. It was not necessary to go into the outside world beyond the landing on the river where the schooner *Nereid* docked with its load of cotton. Sometimes Florilla accompanied Benjamin Bender. She would watch as the bales of cotton were thrown down from the deck, and the finished cloth from the mill was loaded in its place. Touching the ship's hull, she could see the places it had been, the busy ports, the open sea. Near the landing was a grove of pygmy pines, so small that Florilla could reach their upper branches. Running among them, she felt she could touch the sky.

Less commonly, the outside world would come to Benderville. Parties of travelers on horseback sometimes mistook the turning and blundered into the center of the town. One cloudy night in summer, when children were reluctantly starting indoors, an elephant and a camel came straight down Main Street. Fortunov's Traveling Circus, on its way to the resort towns of the coast, had taken a wrong turning. The elephant stood as tall as the houses, taller than some of the trees. Its tread shook the ground. The younger children ran in terror, and the older ones pressed themselves against fences or shinnied up trees. Benjamin Bender stood in its path, demanding that the processions stop. The rider of the elephant, a dark, wizened figure, did not seem to understand much English. But a man in military uniform on a white horse, Captain Fortunov himself, came galloping along the line of carts and animals to confer in a heavy accent with Benjamin Bender, explaining that he traveled by night so that no one should be given a free look at his circus.

Horses whinnied and were answered by the horses and mules of a workaday world. The camel snorted and flapped its long upper lip. The elephant touched the fence delicately, curiously with its trunk. There were foreign words and the exotic pinpoint flares of cigarettes.

When it was explained to Captain Fortunov that he had taken the wrong road, it was necessary for the gates of the mill yard to be thrown open, to make space for the wagons to turn.

Florilla ran to watch. Whips cracked, and the teams moved forward like the night armies she had read about in Caesar's campaigns. The final vehicle was a gypsy wagon something like Munion's. Florilla froze until she saw the painted words: MADAM SCHEHERAZADE, FORTUNE TELLER. As the spotted horse pulled it through the arc of lamplight, Madam Scheherazade nodded toward her, and then, for one moment, Florilla felt a wild pull, a stirring, a longing to run after them. The camel and the elephant turned slowly, carefully and followed.

In the morning, their strange tracks and the heaps of dung were the only evidence that the scene had been real. Small boys stood in the elephant's tracks till workmen came with brooms and rakes to restore Main Street's surface. Florilla followed the hoofprints, the marks of wagon wheels to the end of town, through the stretch of woods to the Tuckerton road where she lost them in the traces of the crowds who had passed there.

But most of the time, Florilla was content with the world as she knew it: the mill, the mansion, her books, lessons with Benjamin Bender each afternoon at five o'clock, and when that grew oppressive, her new friend Fiona and the woods full of demonic tales of outlaws and fugitives. Then there were the even older stories, legends of ghosts and will-o'-the-wisps, of Sammy Buck who out-fiddled the devil, playing the Air Tune, which no one knew but was said to linger in the forest's atmosphere. Or the white stag that appeared to save humans from disaster. Then there was the drama of nature itself: the wild lightning storms of summer, plagues of mosquitoes, fire in the pines. It was all this that filled Florilla's world.

When she parsed the travels of Odysseus, they seemed a journey through a familiar landscape, as if the man of twists and turns had voyaged between the sandy islands off the coast, been cast up at the Wading River, but because he was a Greek, described it differently. Scylla and Charybdis were no stranger than the Jersey Devil, the Air Tune no less powerful than the Sirens' song, and what shack on a swamp hummock might not shelter a Circe?

6

So the years passed, an odd synthesis of work in the mill and the dreams of classical antiquity. As Florilla's eighteenth birthday approached, Benjamin Bender was worried. Her Latin and Greek had progressed apace, and she worked diligently in the cloth room. The cloth room saw the final folding and baling of the finished cloth, quieter, less taxing work than tending the looms of the weave room. He felt that he had had a hand in creating a creature of some rarity and that it was his duty to protect his handiwork. He watched her narrowly when she left the mill in a gaggle of young people. Her friend Fiona had taken up with a young man, and he was afraid that Florilla would throw herself away on some good-looking young factory hand and sacrifice her life to household and babies. It was the way of Benderville.

And then there was Munion. Though he had not come again to Benderville, letters came when he needed money, ill spelled but clear in their purpose. Benjamin Bender complied. There were sightings now and then. In summer, he was often reported in the shore towns, but gradually he seemed to drift up to Long Branch and the bigger resorts close to New York. Some even said that he had been murdered by one of his many enemies as he traveled the back roads of the Pines, perhaps on his way to reclaim Florilla. But these were only stories.

"I've known Munions," old Tom Cranmer said. "They don't die before their time."

Benjamin Bender was uneasy because he knew that Florilla was worth a lot more to the wizard than the bits of money he extorted. She clearly had the ability to ease pain. She would go often to the female boarding house in the evening to help with aching legs, sore backs, and headaches—results of long days in the weave room. He knew, too, that she sometimes accompanied Lethe on her forays into the woods to help the sick and injured on their flight to freedom. Eventually, Munion would hear of it. Benjamin Bender wanted to remove her from danger, even if it meant losing her. He thought of Dr. Peace's story about Florilla's mother. One evening, he asked Florilla her mother's name

Florilla looked up from her Cicero in some surprise.

"Her name was Sarah Siddall," she said.

The Benderville Mill had an office in Philadelphia. It took little doing to find the uncle, Jonathan Siddall, who owned the cottage at Sea Grove. He agreed to speak to his father and mother again. The answer came back quickly. They had no interest in their granddaughter. Their daughter, as far as they were concerned, had never existed. Jonathan Siddall said it was out of his hands. Of this, Benjamin Bender said nothing to Florilla, but one avenue was closed to him.

Florilla was aware of none of this. She lived in her world of dreams where the stories of the ancients were superimposed on her surroundings. The mill's dye house fascinated her. It was next door to the cloth room, so when there was a wait for cloth to come down from the weave room, she would go outside and sit on a bench in the courtyard outside. The dye house doors were always open, and from where she sat, it was as chimerical as Erebos. It swirled with cottony smoke through which she could see the fires burning under the brick dye vats. Often Andrew McKenzie, the dye master, would come to the door like some strange god, naked to the waist and spattered with color, face streaked with soot. Florilla liked to talk to him. He would sit with her sometimes and tell her about his boyhood in a border village in Scotland, his work in the mills of New Lanark.

New Lanark, he explained had been the project of the social reformer Robert Owen. The workers were far better treated at New Lanark than in other British mills. They had better housing and a sickness fund. Children were educated in the ways Benjamin Bender espoused. Benjamin Bender's ideas owed much to Robert Owen, Andrew McKenzie said, but in Benderville he had done so much more.

"It's the small scale," Andrew McKenzie said, "and no history to overcome. He's been able to do it all as he believes."

After coming to America, Andrew McKenzie had first worked at Franklinville, Massachusetts, but as a believer in the theories of Robert Owen, and in the hope of the dawning of a new social order, he had followed Benjamin Bender south to New Jersey.

Florilla thought him a kind man but old. He was thirty-two. He had read a great deal, and they talked about books. Sometimes he went up to Philadelphia, and when he returned, he brought her books.

This friendship was not lost on Benjamin Bender and decided him on a new course of action. Andrew McKenzie was a good man, a solid worker. If he married Florilla, he would keep her safe. He would not mind her studying; they would stay at Benderville, and he himself would still have someone with whom to explore his beloved classics. McKenzie had some education, probably some Latin at least. He would speak to him.

Andrew McKenzie was not averse to the idea, seemed eager in fact, but how to put it to Florilla? Directly, Benjamin Bender decided. And so at dinner he said:

"Now, Florilla, you will be eighteen in a matter of months, and I feel we should discuss your future."

"I'll stay here," Florilla said. "I'll work in the mill. I like it here. And you have told me many times that there is no other factory town like it."

"Of course you may stay here. But you may not always want to live in this house."

"Oh," Florilla said, "I could move to the boarding house, is that what you mean?"

"No, I meant that you might want a house of your own." He cleared his throat. "Might want to marry."

"Marry?" Florilla repeated, bewildered.

Benjamin Bender did not feel equal to his task. He could discuss wages and working conditions, accounts and processes for milling cotton; he could talk about social systems and about community, about religion and education, but matters of the human heart were trackless. He was lost. He gazed at Florilla. He knew that she was at an age when many girls married, and yet, looking at her, he still saw the child brought to him that April day almost seven years before. She had filled out, the face was rounder, though the features were stronger, more distinct. He was glad he had not sent her into the weave room; he had seen too many girls drained of their color, moving with the exhaustion of much older women. He did not, of course, know how to reconcile that undesirable result with the operation of the Benderville Mill. He could not shorten the workday and still compete with other mills. He had to think that this life, even with its drawbacks, was better than a life of drudgery on a starveling farm. He had seen that too: women bound to the harsh cycles of rural life.

Benjamin Bender squared his shoulders; he must not quail. She had come to him with a blasted heritage. In those terms, he was offering her a lot. Like life in the mill, it was a fair compromise. McKenzie was, after all, a good man, a kind man.

"My child," Benjamin Bender began, "I have been empowered—" He stopped.

Florilla looked at him quizzically. Was he getting forgetful? Adolescence had made her painfully aware of the mutability of all things, of age and death.

"Andrew McKenzie," Benjamin Bender said, "has asked me to speak to you."

"He can speak to me himself," Florilla said, surprised. "I see him every day. The dye house is next door to the cloth room."

"This, my dear, is a delicate subject. He did not wish to alarm you."

He paused.

"He has spoken to me several times. He would like to marry you, Florilla."

"*Marry* me?"

Seeing the shock on her face, he spoke quickly.

"He realizes that you are young and is prepared to accept a long engagement."

Florilla crumpled in her chair.

"He's a good man, Florilla," Benjamin Bender said, for she had got to her feet.

"But Mr. Bender," Florilla said, " I don't want to marry anyone. Why can't I go on as I am? Working in the cloth room? Or in the weave room, perhaps, to earn more. I can live in the boarding house, and I'll be no burden to you. I can support myself in the mill! That is the freedom that manufacturing gives. You told me that yourself. You've told me that since I was a child!"

"For the average girl that is true. You are not average. You have an education, an education on which I have spent a not inconsiderable amount of time. For you to toil in the mills for a lifetime would make that worthless."

"I can still read," Florilla said. "If I go on in the cloth room, I have time to read, and I can study at night. You told me the Franklinville girls do that."

"Florilla, Florilla. They are the daughters of Yankee farmers, and the mills are their only chance for education of any kind. I have given you more, much more."

Florilla's face grew stubborn.

"You told me," she said, "the mills were a freedom. Now you say they are a prison. I think *marriage* is a prison. I think it was a prison for my mother."

And with that, she turned to go.

"Florilla, Mr. McKenzie is coming to dinner tomorrow night. I would like you to dine with us. Think over what I've said. He expects no answer immediately. I ask you to be sensible."

Florilla bowed her head.

"I will come to dinner," she said.

Florilla sat at the window of her room. The moon was bright, and she looked down on the careful geometry of the garden. She wouldn't do it. She would not marry an old man. Andrew McKenzie was nearly as old as her own father. She would support herself, if not here, then in another mill town. She cried softly because she felt herself betrayed. First Fiona had betrayed her, going off into the grown-up world with Tom Matthews. Now she was supposed to follow, and not even with someone of her own choosing. She squeezed her eyes shut against the hot tears.

"You come here," Ananda said. "You ain't goin' into dinner with hair all down your back like a little girl."

"Why not?" Florilla tried to pull away from the firm grip on her shoulders.

"Cuz you're growed up now, that's why not. And there's a gennelman to dinner."

Sighing, Florilla held still and allowed Ananda to produce a hair-brush and sweep the mass of hair up on her head, pinning it here and there, stepping back to inspect her work. Florilla wore her new dress, a blue sprigged calico, because Lethe had spirited away all the others.

"If you'd get that wild look out of your eyes," Ananda grumbled, "you'd look like a young lady."

"Who'd've thought," she added, "such a scrawny imp would grow up pretty."

Florilla entered the parlor where the men were sitting. Both stood up. When she had sat down, they continued their conversation about dye-stuffs. This gave Florilla a chance to look critically at Andrew McKenzie. He was dressed in a frock coat and britches. He had scrubbed his hands till they looked red and raw, working hands, awkward in his lap. He was tall enough, and, she knew, strong. He had a rather small-featured face, an undershot jaw, bright, pale blue eyes. His hair, neatly combed tonight, was brown and thick. Fiona had once called him handsome and, really, he was. Still, to Florilla he seemed old, steady and methodical in his thought and his movements.

Watching them both, Benjamin Bender felt even more uneasy. Grown, Florilla was more of a marvel than the brilliant child who devoured everything Mr. Magreavey could give her. Perhaps there was no limiting her. Perhaps he was wrong. *A fish that can sing opera.* Munion's words flashed into his mind, fixing his purpose.

Married, she would be safe from Munion's claims. In fact, McKenzie was a rare find: a man who would appreciate her talents—if she didn't insist on staring at him as though he were some form of life she had never seen before. The poor man looked as flushed and embarrassed as a schoolboy.

"Don't say anything, my dear," said Benjamin Bender when their guest had left. "We won't mention it for a time."

Florilla avoided Andrew McKenzie as much as she could. She no longer spent her spare time sitting outside on the bench but stayed inside the cloth room, protected by the boisterous company. She dreaded the ringing in and the noontime ringing out, for then she was sure to run into him in the mill yard. At the first note of the bell, she would bolt, to the great amusement of her fellow workers. At night, it was easier to avoid him because he stayed late to supervise the dousing of the dye house fires.

He didn't seem aware that she fled from him; perhaps he thought it was some kind of girlish modesty. He became more overt in his gestures. She would come back from lunch to find a posy, a bag of candy. He brought back even more books when he went to town.

The word spread round the village like wildfire: Andrew McKenzie would marry Florilla Munion. A lucky match for her, they said; the old man must have arranged it. Andrew McKenzie was an educated man, and he had standing in the town. The old man must have planned it to keep her there and to keep the wizard off.

"You can't stop a wizard," said the children. "He'll send huge crows to fetch her in the night!"

"He'll send the Jersey Devil!"

They were hushed and shooed away. But even some of the girls in the weave room whispered that Munion would be angry, that he'd put a spell on the wedding.

"Nonsense," said old Tom Cranmer, "Munion ain't no real wizard. Not like his grandfather. That one could make the girls think they was knee deep in water so's they'd lift up their skirts."

As Benderville became more and more certain of the marriage plan, Florilla became more set against it. She found it painful that someone who had been her friend could now fill her with horror. She gave the presents of candy to the bobbin doffers, she threw the flowers into the mill race, even the books she hid away in her cupboard, unopened.

"Remember," Benjamin Bender said to her early in the spring, "this is the only thing that can keep you safe from your father. He will have no rights over you once you have a husband."

"What good is that," said Florilla furiously, "when my husband will? If he can do what he wants with me, how is that different from my father?"

In May, word spread that Munion was back. He had been seen as close as the tavern on the Tuckerton stage road. Drunk, he had been talking about getting the constable and coming to take his daughter back. It was criminal, he said, for her to work in a factory with her talent for the family trade.

"Florilla," Benjamin Bender said, "you must be careful. Let Mr. McKenzie walk you home. Don't go into the woods. I want you to think seriously about setting a date for your marriage."

"Yes, Mr. Bender," Florilla said. She looked at the marble statue of Daphne and envied her.

7

Two nights later, Florilla ran away. She left after everyone was asleep and she knew that the watchman was at the far end of town by the cottages. She ran across Main Street, dodging quickly behind one of the maples. Looking back once at the still, dark house, she flitted across the Wading River bridge and walked in the shadow of the pines to the point where a narrow sand road led into the woods. She wasn't really sure where it came out, for this was not a section of the woods she knew well, which she hoped meant they would not look for her there. The moon was clouded over, but the spring night was warm. She wore her work dress, boots, a shawl. She carried away little more than she had come with: only food and her copy of *The Odyssey*.

Florilla walked for most of the night. She had been afraid that the road might peter out in a collier's clearing, but it went on its crooked way. Near dawn, she climbed a slight rise to find the remains of a burned-out farm. In a barn, on some moldy hay, she slept, waking to a landscape at once familiar and strange.

All around her on the hilltop were strewn blackened stones and charred timber. A shed, half burned, leaned crazily toward the ground. A shallow depression filled with more charred wood showed where the house had stood. Except that there were no trees, the landscape bore few traces of fire. She could see the green beginnings of bushes and scrub that would, by high summer, hide all but the old barn. Florilla had come upon many places like this in her wanderings, and they always filled her with a foreboding loneliness, as though they embodied some truth, some prediction that she could not decipher. So keenly did she feel the lives lived here and abandoned that she was afraid a waking dream might show her some picture of destruction.

She walked to the edge of the hill. From it she could see over acres of pine and oak. She could see the sand roads meandering in all directions, the glinting paths of the rivers, the blue fire of the lakes. She picked up her bundle. No path led down off the hill, but a short distance below she saw another road and struck off for it.

Florilla walked west. By afternoon she had reached the edge of the forest, where the pines began to give way to deciduous trees. She had seen no one, not even the trace of a charcoal fire. As she rounded a bend in the road, she saw that the trees thinned into several grassy clearings before the road became a causeway over a stretch of marsh. In the last of these clearings clustered one of the small herds of cattle that roamed loose in the Pines. They watched her, blowing through their nostrils, as she hurried by. She reached the causeway itself to see a brindled cow with crooked horns standing over a very young calf. Florilla stopped. She knew better than to try to pass. Cows could be dangerous if they thought a calf was threatened. Eventually, nosing and licking, the cow got the little creature to its feet and it made a wobbly progress after her into the trees.. Florilla pressed on.

The causeway crossed the marsh and dwindled into a thicket of cedar trees where it ended altogether in a narrow clearing. Piles of logs here and there suggested that this stand of cedars had been used at some time for lumber. Halting, Florilla was startled to hear a voice close by.

"Damn," the voice said. "Damn and blast."

Florilla stood still. There was a thrashing sound in the cedars near the edge of the clearing. A logger?

"What a bloody nuisance," the voice said.

It couldn't be a logger. This was not the accent of the Pines, was not, in fact, an accent she had ever heard before. Slowly, heart beating fast, she made her way toward the voice. As her eyes got used to the gloom of the cedar thicket, she saw a straw hat glimmering on the moss like a huge pale moth. She tripped over a cloth bound book and a leather bag.

"My God," the voice cried. "My specimens! Bloody cow!"

"I'm not a cow," Florilla retorted.

There was an immediate silence.

"I beg your pardon," said the voice, "but I'm down here half in this wretched swamp and I can't even see you."

Florilla righted the bag, closed the book, and stepped to the lip of the bank. She found herself looking down into the face of a young man. He was lying half in, half out, of the shallow water.

"I wouldn't wade in there," Florilla said. "That's the kind of place you get snappers."

"Snappers?"

"Snapping turtles. Bite your toe off."

"Oh, good God," he said, "this is the most infernally dangerous continent. No, I hardly need that."

And he smiled up at her. Florilla thought that she had never seen a smile so beautiful, like the smile on the face of the young Endymion in a drawing in the library at Benderville, even to the lock of hair falling across his forehead.

"I say," he asked after a moment, "are you a wood nymph?"

Bracing himself on his hands, he tried to draw himself further out of the water, but a look of such pain crossed his face that Florilla, kneeling, asked:

"Are you hurt?"

"Not badly," he answered. "Jolly lucky, really. I managed to get between that bloody cow and her calf. She went for me, and I went over the bank. But she got my left leg a bit with her horn. Not deep. Trying to stop it bleeding."

"Well, sitting in the water won't do you any good," Florilla said.

"Won't it? I thought it might."

He turned over on his stomach and slowly, painfully crawled up on the dry bank. One leg of his linen trousers was torn and bloodied.

"Lie down flat," Florilla said.

"Scissors in my bag," said the young man.

With these, Florilla cut the cloth away to reveal a long gash in the calf, bleeding but beginning to clot.

"Can't move my arm well," he said. "Might have sprained my shoulder too."

"Just lie there."

"Now don't you get bitten by a snapper," he called after her as she went down the bank.

Florilla returned with handfuls of sphagnum moss. With this, she had once seen Indian Mary dress a similar wound. She cut the ruined trouser leg into strips, packed the moss into the cut and bound it up.

"Lie still," she said, gently tracing the length of the bound wound with the palm of her hand.

"Well," said the young man weakly, "you're not a nymph. Nymphs are useless creatures. I think you must be an angel. My leg was burning like fire and now that's stopped."

"Do you live near here?" he asked.

Florilla shook her head.

"That's a pity. Neither do I. And how in the devil am I to get home?"

"How did you get here?" Florilla asked practically.

"Canoe. It's pulled up on the bank over the other side."

"Where are you going?"

"Difficult to explain. But I know the way. What about you?"

Florilla sighed.

"Not anywhere, really."

"Not anywhere? How jolly interesting."

He closed his eyes and said ruefully.

"Even if I could drag myself over to the canoe, not sure I could paddle. Shoulder's a bit useless."

Florilla sat cross-legged on the moss, considering.

"I can paddle a canoe," she said finally.

"What? A girl? All by yourself? With a weight like me in it?"

"Of course."

"Well," he said, "you're neither angel nor nymph, you're a woodswoman. I should introduce myself. My name is Colin Drysdale, and yours?"

Florilla thought quickly.

"Flora," she said. "Flora Homer."

They sat in silence for a time.

"My leg feels much better," he said.

He sat up.

"Now look, Flora," he said, "do you think you could bring me my specimen case? I do want to be sure everything's there. It's a marvel that blithering cow didn't trample it."

"There now," he opened it with his good hand. "Looks all right. Let's see. *Epigaea repens. Drosera filiformis. Minuartia caroliniana. Lycopodium carolinianum.*"

"Why do you use the Latin names?" Florilla asked.

"Good heavens," the young man said, "you know that's Latin? Gracious! I am a botanist. Thus, when talking to myself, I use the Latin names."

He continued talking to himself, shaking his head.

"Still no *Schizaea pusilla*. And that's what I came to this confounded swamp to find."

Florilla frowned.

"*Schizaea pusilla*. Split tiny?"

"Greek too! Formidable! But the plant is perhaps known to you as the curly grass fern."

"But that is tiny," Florilla said. "You can never see it in the spring. Sometimes in winter because it's evergreen and it stands out."

"Yes," he said. "I know. That's why I was crawling about on my stomach. I never saw the cow, never mind the calf. I'm not sure I can wait for winter."

"I'll get you to the canoe," Florilla said, "then I'll come back for your hat and your book and your specimen case."

"Will you?" he said uncertainly. "Perhaps you should take them first."

"That would be stupid," said Florilla. "I don't even know where the canoe is. I could spend hours beating my way through thickets."

"Yes," he said. "Yes, I do see. I expect you're right."

She helped him to his feet. Standing, he was tall and thin and it was not easy for him to lean on her, so they made a crippled progress to the other side of the clearing where the canoe was moored to a huge cedar knee. Florilla took off her stockings and boots and flung them into the boat. Wading out, she got him seated in the bow.

Florilla went back to the clearing and picked up the book. Surreptitiously opening it to the flyleaf, she read:

Colin Drysdale
Magdalen College
Oxford

This meant nothing to her, but it made her intensely curious. She picked up the hat and the bag and carried them back to the canoe. Hiking up her skirts, she waded into the water, untied the painter, and jumped neatly into the stern.

Colin Drysdale watched with admiration as Florilla, kneeling as Indian Mary had taught her, maneuvered the boat through the swamp. The dappled light touched sometimes the golden hair, sometimes the look of serious concentration on the young face. She pushed off from the underwater roots of the cedar trees till they passed the edges of the shade into open marsh.

A maze of creeks threaded among grassy islets. Florilla shaded her eyes against the lowering sun. In the bow, the young man was turned away from her.

"Now," he said, "keep to the right along the bigger creek and I'll tell you what to do."

The creek meandered for a short distance through some pines, then into a wider creek that emptied in turn into a small shallow pond clotted with yellow water lilies.

"Just right," Colin Drysdale said. "Now we cross this pond and there'll be a small creek leading out of it. We follow that."

At first, it was hard to see the entrance to the creek.

"To the left," he called, "just by the *kalmia!*"

"Do you mean the laurel?" Florilla asked a little crossly. Though she was a strong paddler, the days in the cloth room had lessened her endurance, and an early evening wind made the going heavy.

"That's it. Laurel. Are you exhausted? We could stop for a bit, you know. Florilla shook her head.

The canoe nosed through the tangle of brush into a small, fast-flowing branch. Here the going, with the current, was much easier, although at times it was perilously narrow and overhung by a network of branches. They traveled a long way down the creek, dodging submerged logs and gravel sandbars.

"I'll be able to take you home tomorrow morning in the carriage," Colin Drysdale ventured.

"I'm not going home," Florilla replied.

After that, there was silence save for the smooth plash of the paddle, branches brushing against the hull.

"Duck your head," she said as they passed under a low-branched oak.

"Look here," he said, "are you running away?

"That's my business," Florilla said shortly.

"My dear girl, you have done something very like save my life. I am hardly looking for an excuse to hand you over to some authority. I am quite certain that you can stay at Woodland Place as long as you like."

Florilla had never heard of anywhere called Woodland Place, but she knew the Pines stretched a distance beyond Benderville.

The creek began to widen, the current slowed, the branches drew back. About a mile later, they rounded another bend into a stretch of brilliant light, the glow of the setting sun.

"Ah," Colin Drysdale said, "now here we are. There's the house."

Florilla looked up. Sun lingered on a sweeping green lawn sloping up from the riverbank, edged by shadowy rhododendron bushes. At the top of the lawn was a building like a Greek temple, sculpted pediment and entablature, huge white columns, the whole tinged with the roseate sunset light, the same light that glowed from the tall windows. She saw also a number of outbuildings of a more Gothic fancy, turrets and roofs of red clay tile, stone walls overgrown with ivy, the woods crowding up behind them.

From the terrace behind the columns, two children, a boy and a girl, came running, followed by two hysterically barking spaniels. The foursome fairly tumbled down the lawn, the children calling "Colin! Colin!"

"Here," Colin said to Florilla, if you can bring it in to the dock, Julian will tie it up. I say, well done! Here we are. This is Woodland Place."

Woodland Place

Summer 1855

8

As the children neared, shouting and waving, two swans emerged from the closest rhododendron bushes and swam regally away. Florilla was awed by the dreamlike nature of the place. Was she still asleep in the abandoned barn, or even in her bed at Benderville?

"It *is* real, you know," Colin Drysdale said. "It's a bit of a surprise in the middle of the forest."

The boy, Julian, seemed to be about nine. He threw himself down on the dock, grabbed the painter and expertly tied it up. He didn't seem in the least surprised to see a second person in the canoe.

The girl, a year or two younger, capered up and down the dock, keening to herself. She was most eccentrically dressed in pantaloons and a velvet basque. Several bright feathers of a plumage Florilla had never encountered were stuck in her tangle of dark curls.

"You're wounded," the boy said, looking down into the canoe. His accent had traces of Colin's. There was a look of Colin about him altogether. The same lock of wavy chestnut hair fell across his forehead, and he narrowed the same fine hazel eyes to look at Colin's leg.

"Rosabel!" Julian said. "Go get someone! Mr. Jade or someone!"

"He's writing in the tower," Rosabel said. "I'd have to throw gravel at the window. And Boffin took Mama off to the ruin to do sketches for *The Flight of Guinevere*."

"Well, go to the stables then and get someone. Oh, never mind, I'll go."

He was off, running.

Rosabel sat down on the dock.

"Show me your wound," she said breathlessly.

"Did the lady bandage it?" she asked after a moment's staring.

"Yes," said Colin, "she did and more."

Rosabel considered Florilla.

"What is your name then?" asked Rosabel.

Florilla looked her straight in the eye.

"Flora," she said. "Flora Homer."

"What an odd name."

"Don't be rude, Rosabel." Colin bent one of his wonderful smiles on Florilla. "I think it's charming."

By this time, there was activity up at the house: voices, banging doors. Julian appeared at the top of the lawn with a posse including an old man in clerical robes.

"Oh, Lord," Colin groaned. "Father Floreat. Come to mumble a few words in case I'm on the way out."

"Is there a church here?" Florilla asked.

"Chapel. My aunt went over to the Romans. Father Floreat's her pet priest."

Since Roman to Florilla meant pagan, she was left to puzzle it out as several burly workmen descended on the canoe. She was lifted out bodily, Colin after her. He was carried easily up the lawn.

"Good gracious," Father Floreat kept saying, "my dear boy did you meet a savage plant?"

"A cow actually," Colin said without further explanation.

Before his leg was unbound or the doctor sent for, Colin insisted that Florilla be taken upstairs and brought some tea. Florilla's first thought was that she would slip away during the confusion, but the room in which she found herself made what she had thought splendid at Benderville seem spare.

It was at the front of the house, its huge windows giving on lawn and river, a large, high-ceilinged room, painted the blue of an October sky.

All around the walls, just under the white ceiling, ran a frieze of mythical beasts: griffins, unicorns, hippocampi, painted in grisaille. The furniture was fragile and gilded, unlike the heavy mahogany furniture of Benjamin Bender's house. The bed was made in the shape of a swan. The walls were covered with paintings, landscapes and still lives, in gold frames. The curtains at the window and the bedcover were of a polished material that she had never seen before, intricately patterned with pale pink roses and wide blue ribbons. Amid peace and beauty, she lay down on the bed and fell asleep.

Lady Amberwell knocked lightly on the bedroom door. When there was no answer, she was tempted to imagine, but for the testimony of children and servants, that the beautiful golden-haired girl was a figment of Colin's imagination, the hallucination of shock. She pushed the door open and, indeed, there the girl was, stretched out on the swan bed, fast asleep, golden hair splayed over the pillow. A nymph. A perfect Daphne. She closed the door and flew down the passage to Boffin's room.

"Boffin!" she cried, knocking urgently on the door. "Colin has brought you your Daphne!"

Florilla awoke to see two people staring down at her. One was a youngish man in a painter's smock, dark haired, dark bearded with an intense and pudgy face. The other was a very beautiful woman of perhaps thirty with hair of a rare dark auburn hanging in two heavy plaits threaded through with gold-and-silver cord. She was wearing a shapeless gown of green velvet, and on her head was a golden crown. Florilla sat up staring.

"Now don't be frightened," Lady Amberwell said, and her voice was American. "Why are you staring?"

"It could be," said the young man in an accent like Colin's, "because you are still dressed as Guinevere."

She reached up and removed the crown.

"Oh, of course. I'm sorry. I have been sitting for Mr. Hunt all afternoon, and I was just on my way to change."

"She is a perfect Daphne," the young man said. "Quite perfect."

Daphne, Florilla thought desperately. If only I could become a tree.

"Well, never mind about that now," said Lady Amberwell as Florilla's eyes widened in panic. "Go on, Boffin."

The young man left. Lady Amberwell sat down on the bed beside Florilla.

"My dear," she said, pushing Florilla's hair back from her forehead with a cool, white hand, "I am most tremendously grateful to you for rescuing my nephew. I don't know what would have become of him had you not happened by. Certainly we wouldn't have found him for days. Or known where to look. Even I, who spent a lot of my childhood here, lose my way in the woods. And, of course, being English, he doesn't understand the dangers."

When Florilla did not seem to respond, she continued.

"I don't know where you were going when you found my nephew, but he must have taken you a long way out of your way. Since it is late, I would like to ask you to stay the night, and we will make arrangements to take you home in the morning. Or," and here she looked at Florilla shrewdly, "will people be worried about you?"

Florilla shook her head.

"I left home," she said.

"Ah," said Lady Amberwell, "I see."

A maid brought pitchers of water and a hip bath. She also brought soap and towels and a dress of white lawn.

"Her ladyship thought this would fit you."

Bathed and dressed by the sounding of the dinner gong, Florilla descended the wide, curving staircase into the central hall, which ran the width of the house from the river lawn to the front door that faced the carriage driveway and the rose gardens.

At the foot of the stairs, she hesitated. She could hear voices, but she didn't know which way to go. A man servant in livery carrying a tray came through one of the pairs of high double doors. Florilla stared, never having seen anyone so costumed.

"In there," he said to her with disdain, throwing open the other double doors.

As she entered the room, she was aware of candlelight, an elaborate mantel between long, curtained windows, paintings, pillars, and a number of people grouped in front of the fireplace, where, since the evening was cold, pine logs snapped and flared. Colin called her name and she saw him sitting in an armchair, leg supported by a footstool.

"This is Flora," he said, "the girl who saved me."

There was a general murmur of appreciation.

"Now," Colin said, "you have met my aunt, Lady Amberwell and Father Floreat."

Father Floreat raised his hand as if dispensing a blessing.

"This is my old friend, Prosper Hunt, called Boffin, a painter."

The bearded young man who had called her Daphne bowed toward her.

"Freeman Jade, our resident poet and novelist."

He indicated a rotund little man dressed in black who nodded his head and blinked nervously. There were two others, a Miss Euphemia

Potts, naturalist and bat expert, and a lanky, haunted looking man, Dr. Alcock, a composer.

"This," said Lady Amberwell expansively, "is the core of our little household at present. We have a great many other visitors much of the time."

"Don't frighten her, Aunt Lou," Colin said, for Florilla, in the white dress, seemed poised for flight, like an unwilling bride.

When dinner was announced, they crossed the hall to the dining room, another enormous room extending the entire width of the house. The long table blazed with huge silver candelabras. More candles in sconces on the wall cast a flickering light over an unfinished mural of mythical scenes. Some figures were only sketched in, and on one wall there was scaffolding. She thought, at first, that the two parrots on a perch in a dark corner were part of the painting until they screeched, flapped their wings, and one of them shrieked.

"Art! Food!"

"My pets," said Lady Amberwell, blowing them a kiss.

"Boffin did those paintings," said Colin, who sat opposite Florilla. "They are mythological scenes with an American background."

And, sure enough, there was Europa fondling one of the very red-and-white bulls that roamed the Pines, Actaeon, painted only half way up his athletic torso, parting the branches of a sweet pepper bush to spy on the naked Diana, who, even in chalk, was immediately recognizable as Lady Amberwell. They all disported on a minutely detailed carpet of local flora.

The unfinished figures reminded Flora of how she felt, half in, half out of reality. Occasionally, as she studied which unfamiliar knife or fork to use, she would look up to see Colin smiling encouragement and tactfully holding up the right one. The conversation at the table was also entirely different from the rather ponderous exchanges held over dinner at Benderville. Here, everyone seemed to talk at once; here was no rumination between question and answer, no silences while feats of mental arithmetic involving bales bought and yardage produced took place. There were theories aplenty, but because they were just theories, unattached to the hard realities of production and cost, they flew like birds.

Miss Potts, a wiry little woman who smoked a cheroot over coffee, expounded her theory that the Jersey Devil was, in fact, a huge antipodal bat that had made the trip to America from Australia in some unknown fashion. To capture the creature would be a tremendous addition to the understanding of animal migration.

Boffin discoursed on the power of art to educate taste. Lady Amberwell took up the need for America to realize the importance of art and artists, to subsidize them, for only they could bring humanity and hope to this new age of the machine.

Mr. Jade, the writer, addressed himself largely to his plate, commenting only occasionally.

"When I lived in Italy," he said mournfully, "the baker gave me free bread because I was a poet."

The composer said nothing at all. He looked as though he were trying to hear a sound of a frequency beyond the mingled voices, the chinking of silver and glass and china.

"Don't worry," Colin said to Florilla across the table. "They all talk at once, but they're quite harmless."

At this point, the two parrots were brought to the table where they picked fruit out of the centerpiece and ate it sloppily. Florilla could see the provenance of Rosabel's red, blue, and green feathers.

Lady Amberwell, absently stroking a parrot, said that she was tired of the incessant importation of English poets to lecture on the American circuit.

"Where," she cried, "are our native poets?"

Freeman Jade smiled self-deprecatingly and helped himself to an apple.

"Where are your landscape painters?" thundered Boffin. "With all this?"

He gestured at the curtained windows behind him.

Colin laughed.

"They left it all for you, Boffin," he said.

.

9

O n her first morning at Woodland Place, Florilla still expected the factory bell to ring in the day, to order and punctuate it. But now, as for the next few days, she would wake, dress, and go downstairs to find the house empty and silent save for the muffled sounds of breakfast preparation in the kitchens. Wandering outside down the long driveway of crushed oyster shell, toward the stables, she would hear the horses stamping in their stalls as the grooms threw down hay. The stables themselves looked like another house, built of stone with mullioned windows round a courtyard where a seahorse fountain played constantly into a watering trough.

She would wander past Freeman Jade's tower where drawn curtains behind the leaded windows proclaimed him asleep. The only person abroad at that hour was Dr. Alcock, the composer, who would appear out of the woods with an expectant, listening expression. Sometimes he would be playing the organ in the chapel, a small, clapboard building that housed Woodland Place's only bell, a bell for Sundays.

Florilla, who had never been inside a church, liked the interior of the chapel, particularly the multicolored light cast by the stained-glass windows. The pews were of fruitwood, ornately carved, and there were embroidered hassocks to kneel on. Florilla supposed that these were the work of Lady Amberwell. Often after dinner, while conversation raged, she would get out her embroidery frame and stitch silken lilies.

"Well, I think it's extraordinary," Lady Amberwell said. "Here I am in the middle of nowhere, thinking that I will have to go through all the trouble of finding the children a tutor in Philadelphia—advertisements and dreadful weekend visits by prospective candidates—and Colin collects this amazing girl who knows more Latin and Greek than Father Floreat. In a cedar swamp! She takes Virgil and Thucydides up to read in bed!"

Dressed as Guinevere again, she was posing beside the old blast furnace. Boffin, dressed entirely in white and wearing a straw hat, was working on the last details of the large canvas.

"We must keep her," he said. "I want to use her in the mural as Daphne, and in my *Going West*, the story of the pioneers."

"Yes," Lady Amberwell said vaguely. "I wonder where she came from."

❧ ⁓⁓ ☙

The household at Woodland Place fascinated Florilla. *Household* was really the wrong word. It was, in fact, a community as much as Benderville was. The commodity here was thought, and that, Florilla discovered, was spun in those Gothic outbuildings she had first noticed, buildings which provided living space for a variety of scholars and artists.

From Colin, she learned that Woodland Place had been built by Lady Amberwell's father, Josiah Carroll, near the site of Alice Furnace, the forge he owned that had produced ironware from the Pines bog iron. In the years of the forge's prosperity, the family had spent winters in Philadelphia and summers in the Pines, filling the house with visitors from June to September. Josiah Carroll would also come in spring and fall to look things over and to hunt and fish. The family had still come for a few years after the furnace blew out for the last time, but, finally, the house was closed, left with only a caretaker living over the stables.

When his daughter, Louisa, touring Europe, had met and married Colin's uncle, the young Lord Amberwell, later British Consul at Philadelphia, her father had settled on her the house at Alice Furnace and his substantial landholdings in the Pines. Lord Amberwell had fallen in love with the place for its abundant hunting and fishing. Spring and fall again saw parties of sportsmen: businessmen, diplomats, visiting Englishmen, local political figures.

Lady Amberwell stayed in the house from April to October and occasionally during the rest of the year. It made no difference, Colin told Florilla, whether she was there or not. The house was kept open, the staff remained, and the various scholars and artists she had befriended continued their work in the outbuildings Lord Amberwell had built for overflow houseguests.

"She likes it here much better than she does Philadelphia. This is her little world, and she is queen of it. She only goes to Philadelphia to do the entertaining for my uncle. This year she wants to leave the children here. She thinks the climate's healthier."

"What will you do?"

"Oh," said Colin brightly, "I shall travel. I'm just down from Oxford, and I've been given a purse to study botany of North America, at least the eastern part. I shall have to write up a field report on everything I've seen."

"In the Pines?"

"In as much of the country as I can see, though the Pines are extremely interesting botanically."

Florilla was surprised to feel her heart sink at the thought that any day he might go.

"What are you thinking?" Colin asked.

They were walking down the driveway, its oyster shell surface glittering in the afternoon light. Colin limped slowly; his leg was still stiff.

"I'm thinking," Florilla said to her surprise, "that I should go."

"Go? Whatever for? You've only been here six days."

"But I don't know your aunt," Florilla said. "There is no reason she should let me live here."

"I don't see why not," Colin said cheerfully. "I believe Miss Potts came for a few days last August and she's still here. I could train you to be my assistant, Boffin wants to paint you, and Aunt Lou is most impressed by your knowledge of Latin and Greek. She will need a tutor for the children if they stay here.

"And besides," he added, "I'm not sure you should be off trotting around alone. God knows what you might meet. Even the Jersey Devil, antipodal bat or whatever it is."

They walked on for a little way.

"Besides," he said, "this place in summer is quite a circus. We will be visited by every theorist you can imagine. My aunt runs to art, but my uncle likes social reformers."

"Will you go back to England?"

He said nothing for a few minutes. A cardinal flashed across their path.

"I suppose so," he said. "Yes. I shall have to go back eventually. One does. Shan't you have to go back wherever you came from? You must have a home. You can't really have sprung from the trees."

Florilla wondered if she did have a home. The shack in the woods was her grandmother's retreat from the world. At Benderville, it seemed, she had been a visitor.

"I don't think I do," she answered finally.

"Well then," Colin said, "all the more reason to stay with us."

That night after dinner, they played cards. Once she learned the games, Florilla realized that she won easily because she seemed to know what was in everyone's hands. She thought of her father's card tricks and it frightened her. Feigning sleepiness, she excused herself early.

Alone in her room, she went to the open window, pulled back the chintz curtains, and stared for a long time at the river. The night was clear and the moon three-quarters full. She could hear the whispering leaves of the red oaks that surrounded the house.

Woodland Place seemed like another country, one of which she was neither native nor invited guest. She was her father's daughter, a gypsy stealing others' hearths. She thought of Benjamin Bender's kindness. She had trained in the mill; she should go out into the world to work. But just these few days had made the blank hours in the cloth room repugnant.

There was a light knock and the door opened.

"May I come in?" said Lady Amberwell.

"Of course," said Florilla.

Lady Amberwell was wearing peasant costume, a confection of striped satin and fluttering multicolored ribbons. She looked like a gypsy herself.

"Come," Lady Amberwell said, sitting down on the bed.

Florilla sat down, inhaling a scent like the exhalation of the whole garden at Benderville.

"Now," she said, "I understand from Colin that you think you should leave us. I expect you feel restless, as though you have no place in this household.

"I do understand that," she continued as Florilla began to protest, "and I have a position to offer you. I intend to leave the children at Woodland Place this year while I go back and forth to Philadelphia. I shall need someone who can give them lessons. You are, I think, just what I am looking for."

She pushed Florilla's hair back, taking the heavy weight of it in her hands and piling it up.

"Combs, I think," she said.

10

That summer, Florilla did not have to give lessons because Lady Amberwell wanted the children to be free to roam the countryside.

"Colin," she said, "can give them botany walks, and Miss Potts will do nature things."

As soon as his leg and shoulder had mended, Colin set out to gather specimens of every orchid growing in the Pine Barrens.

"There are," he said to Florilla, "more than twenty species."

Lady Amberwell had decreed that Colin was no longer to go off in the canoe alone; Florilla was to go with him.

"She is clearly," said Lady Amberwell, "more use in the woods than anyone else."

"What is Oxford?" Florilla asked Colin, as they sat, picnic spread about them, on a sandy bank.

"Oxford?" Colin said dreamily. He was examining, under his magnifying glass, the blossom of a bog twayblade orchid.

"Do look," he said, "the petals are most beautifully frilled."

Florilla had rarely seen such joy on any face.

"Look," he breathed, wanting to share the mystery. "Do look. I'll hold the glass."

The orchid's bloom was like a tiny, particular geography of silken ridges and green dapplings.

"Oh," Florilla said, "it is beautiful. It looks like a whole landscape in itself."

"Did you see that?" he said, delighted. "You *did* see that. That's what I see. They are tiny worlds."

"What is Oxford?" Florilla asked again as he carefully put the orchid in the flower press.

"It's a university. In England."

"What is a university?"

"What is a university?" Colin laughed. "How can you know enough Latin and Greek to get a place at one and not know what one is?"

Florilla flushed.

"This isn't England," she said angrily. "Maybe we don't have them."

"Oh, yes, you do. But never mind. I didn't mean to make fun. They are schools, but very advanced schools, that you go to after you've gone to ordinary schools or had tutors for years. You sit an examination when you're about seventeen." He cocked his head to one side. "About your age, in fact. If you pass, you get in."

"Can girls go?"

Colin looked bemused.

"No," he said. "No, I don't suppose they can."

"Why not?'

"Well, I don't know. I never really thought about it. Maybe girls can go in this country."

"Tell me about it," Florilla said.

Lying back against the trunk of a white cedar, Colin described it: the colleges, the quads, the golden stone, the River Cherwell, the bridges, the botanical gardens. He talked until they realized that the sun was lowering, and it was time to start home. As they paddled from creek to creek, the air full of evening birdsong, Colin had the oddest feeling that he was punting on that very Cherwell.

"I almost heard it," Dr. Alcock said sadly at dinner. "I was deep in the woods, and I heard a trill—the first few notes, then it was gone."

He was talking about the Air Tune, the tune that, according to local legend, Fiddler Sammy Buck played for the Devil to save himself from hell. It was a tune the Devil had never heard before and no one had heard since.

"When I find it," Dr. Alcock said, "it will be the basis for my *Pinelands Symphony*."

Colin smiled at Florilla.

Looking at the mural, Florilla saw that Boffin had been at work. Actaeon was complete and Diana now had Lady Amberwell's titian hair and pearly skin.

"We did a lot of work today," Boffin said heartily.

The nights became warmer, and Euphemia Potts announced her intention to begin her bat hunts. She went into the woods at dusk in a small cart pulled by a pony and hung with lanterns to attract insects. In the cart was her paraphernalia, nets on poles like huge butterfly nets and large amounts of extra netting. She, herself, wore a further arrangement of netting over her head.

"Completely mad," Boffin said as she left, a stocky determined figure swallowed almost immediately by the darkness of the trees. They watched the lanterns swinging on the cart till even they disappeared around a bend.

"The Jersey Devil will probably catch her," Julian said with interest.

"If the mosquitoes don't eat her alive."

"Avanti!" Euphemia Potts's voice drifted back to them.

Colin whistled the first notes of a march.

Instantly, Dr. Alcock's head appeared in the lighted window of his studio. "What was that?" he called. "Did you hear that?"

June brought skies full of racing clouds and a profusion of flowers in both wood and garden. The rhododendrons were drenched in blossom, while the woods were laden with the scent of swamp azalea.

Colin and Florilla tramped through field and wood, paddled down rivers and across marshes. Orchids grew, Colin explained to her, in many different terrains, in woods, bogs, swamps. and meadows. Some, like the lady's slipper, were easy to find, but looking for others was like looking for mythical creatures, botanical unicorns.

One day they found a stand of brilliant pink orchids in a swampy meadow.

"*Calpogon pulchellus,*" Colin cried.

Together they knelt over the stalks of rosy blossom. A blue butterfly lit on the flower between them, swaying back and forth. The world seemed suddenly to have fallen silent. The butterfly flew away. Each day brought a different orchid. Florilla would always remember the days by their names: rose pogonia, *arethusa*, helleborine, crane fly.

Colin had been right: summer brought many visitors to Woodland Place, and Lord Amberwell arrived at last. He was a genial man, tall, fair, with the features of a classic Greek statue. He went, as Lady Amberwell put it, with the house. He was, however, concerned with the diplomatic world he moved in, and while tolerant of the eccentricities at Woodland Place, not much interested in them. When he came, he brought with him men of the world, of commerce, law, government, the envoys of other European countries. They shot game in the woods; they fished in the rivers and lakes.

"Not more ducks," Lady Amberwell would say. "Not more bass. Cook will be overcome."

The other side of Lord Amberwell was his passion for social theories. It had made him very happy to be posted to America, where he felt unencumbered by the past with its gray, heavy institutions, its class struggle, even its culture. He wanted to read American writers, to look at American paintings of the frontier. He was bored by Boffin's Pre-Raphaelitism. He might have vetoed the dining room mural if not for its use of local flora and fauna. (If he recognized his wife in the naked Diana, he gave no sign.)

Florilla, between plant hunting trips, met a Cherokee Indian chief; the governor of Pennsylvania; several university professors; Philadelphians of vast fortunes and, sometimes, vast accomplishments; Italian, French, German, and Spanish diplomats and noblemen; Fourierists, Owenites, and utopian socialists of every stripe. Not infrequently, there were visiting English scholars, philosophers, poets, and novelists. These made Freeman Jade very nervous. Florilla thought she would never become used to this exotic parade. Sometimes it made her think of the night the circus came to Benderville.

Florilla and Colin took Julian and Rosabel on botanical walks to the ruins of the iron furnace. Colin liked to show them plants like ebony spleenwort that were not indigenous to the woods.

"It couldn't grow here naturally," Colin said. "There isn't enough lime in the soil. Once man builds with lime, the spores get here from remarkable distances."

Julian and Rosabel teetered from stone to stone of the crumbled ruins.

"Miss Potts showed us the golden crest flower the other day," Julian said. "She says it's disjunct. Its nearest relative is in Australia. She thinks the antipodal bat brought the seeds."

When Lord Amberwell was in residence, Florilla found conversation at the dinner table even more chaotic and incomprehensible. There was much talk of the relationship between Europe and America. There was talk, too, about America itself, about the North and the South, careful talk that usually did not begin till the company had withdrawn to the drawing room for coffee. Florilla liked to pass around the nuts and liqueurs because it allowed her to pick up scraps of conversation. The subjects could be anything from the price of gold to the poems of Wordsworth, and often the talk would turn, hushed and serious to the troubles between North and South. Many of the Quaker visitors were abolitionists, and they talked of underground railroad stops throughout the state including the Pines. Florilla thought of Lethe, but she said nothing. She listened to utopian socialists discussing the failure of Brook Farm, in New England, to make the change from the old transcendentalist ideas to the teachings of Charles Fourier. Some of them had recently stopped at the North American Phalanx at Red Bank, in serious decline since the fire the year before. The land, it appeared, would have to be sold to pay the colony's debts. Like Brook Farm, it had been formed according to Fourier's ideas, though imperfectly expressed. Fourier had imagined all members of the community living in one large building called a phalanstery. At Red Bank, most had still lived in separate cabins. There was a general agreement that vying for individual benefits was so strongly bred into the American character that a truly Fourieristic community could not survive. Lord Amberwell was disappointed by this view.

"You tell me," he would say, "so young a country has so formed a character? I will not believe it."

"Look around you," said one of the recent visitors to Red Bank, "at the men who are here tonight. They have succeeded as individuals, and they are aware that they succeeded alone. The American creed is 'help yourself.'"

Often, Florilla and Colin would slip out onto the terrace.

"Phew," he would say, "it's thick with ideas in there."

And they would go to sit in the rose garden.

"You should smell the roses in England," Colin said more than once. "So much more scent. It's the weather. Everything smells less here because of the heat and because there's not as much rain."

Florilla moved through the days at Woodland Place in a continual state of wonder. If Benderville had been the antithesis of Sim Place, then this was the antithesis of Benderville. There life had been totally ordered and predictable, timed by the schedule of the mill, measured by the ringing of bells: the mill bell, the school bell, which on Sundays became the church bell. Here the days were entirely unpredictable. Picnics and excursions to the shore were mounted at a moment's notice. Dances were decided on a few days beforehand, musicians brought from Philadelphia, drawing rooms cleared of furniture and massed with flowers. On those nights, the gardens glowed with candles while the tremulous chords of the violins arced out into the trees.

Dances were usually held when there was a big house party, and there would be other girls, daughters of the bankers, the diplomats, the merchants. Florilla watched anxiously as Colin danced with them, although he seemed simply to do it in the cheerful, unconcerned fashion with which he did everything.

There were so many amusements. There were games of charades and *tableaux vivants*. The children loved these, for they were often kept up to play fauns or angels. There were evenings of character readings, either of palms or the Tarot. Florilla stopped taking part in the endless games of whist to avoid pretending that she couldn't divine what cards the other players held.

The orchid hunts continued. They were gathering the green fringed orchid, *Habenaria lacera*.

Florilla touched the spidery flowers.

Colin watched her. He had thought her beautiful when he first saw her, but Florilla grew more beautiful each time he looked at her. She even rivaled *Habenaria lacera*.

She glanced up at him.

"Flora," Colin said and faltered. "I don't know what I ever—what I'd do without you. Could you get me the flower press while I write the place and description in the book?"

Had he really said he couldn't do without her? Florilla treasured the words.

"Flora," Boffin said when they got back, "I'm ready to start *Going West*."

"And," he added, "I've had a clever thought. Colin, old man, you as the frontiersman."

"Oh, God, Boffin," Colin said, "I haven't time for that sort of nonsense."

"Yes, you have. I want dawn light. So you two only have to pose at dawn in the woods for an hour three or four times."

For a week, in the first light of dawn, the trio trekked some distance into the woods to a grassy clearing near the forge ruins. They made a strange procession: Boffin striding along leading a mule on which easel, paints, and canvas were strapped, Colin dressed in buckskin, and Florilla wrapped in a blue velvet cloak.

"It's a good thing we're doing this early in the morning," Colin said. "Otherwise we'd faint from the heat."

"You look terribly authentic," Boffin said after everything was set up. "Now stand as close together as possible. Colin, hold her hand, and look back at the ruins."

Boffin sketched furiously. There was silence save for the tentative waking songs of the birds and the scrubbing of the brush.

Florilla was acutely aware of their bodies touching. Through velvet and leather, she thought she could feel the warmth of his skin. She seemed to float in a haze. It was very like the feeling she had had on hot days in the mill. Was this how Fiona felt about Tom Matthews?

Colin squinted at that familiar profile. How many times had they been as close as this, thrashing through swamps, examining flowers, and he been unaware? No, not unaware. Only he couldn't fall in love with her. It just wasn't possible the way things were.

Boffin, moving cumbrously, all his deftness in his hands, thought how beautiful they were, chestnut hair and golden hair and pale skin, thought of legends, thought of myths, thought of the sugared beauty of "The Eve of St. Agnes," wondered briefly if he, like his friend Rosetti, should write poems.

11

A few weeks later, Lady Amberwell gave a costume ball. Although a large house party was already staying, carriages full of people arrived steadily. Lord and Lady Amberwell presided as Apollo and Venus. The children were allowed to stay up and appear, covered in paper leaves, as the Babes in the Wood.

"A beauty," said the Principe di Pontormo, dressed as Dante and talking to Lord Amberwell. He was describing not Lady Amberwell but Florilla. "Wherever did she come from?"

"Out of the woods," said Lord Amberwell. "No one knows more than that. Reads Latin and Greek. Always wins at cards."

The Principe laughed incredulously.

Any number of young men danced with Florilla, but she only noticed that Colin did not. As her dance card filled, she saw him several times with Fanny Greenough.

Fanny Greenough, a cousin of Lady Amberwell's, was part of the house party. Florilla knew that Colin found her amusing because she had lived for a while at the North American Phalanx at Red Bank and still espoused Fourier's wilder theories. Florilla thought her pretty, with her dark curls and high coloring. She had an offhand, merry sort of sophistication. She had told stories at dinner the night before about life at the Phalanx. Florilla might know Latin and Greek, but she was aware that she was, in the ways of Woodland Place, unfinished.

On that evening, without being sure of it, she danced with her second cousin. His name was Gervase Siddall. She recognized her mother's name but to ask would have been to give herself away. The night was hot, so they went out onto the terrace where tables were set with smudge pots to keep the mosquitoes away. Huge moths beat themselves against the lighted windows. With unerring precision, bats dove between the columns and snatched them up.

"Here," Colin called, "over here."

Florilla and Gervase sat with him and Fanny Greenough while she regaled them with more stories of the Phalanx.

"However," Fanny said, "though I may make it sound funny, I am sorry it didn't last." Her eyes grew wide and earnest. "You can't imagine how wonderful it is when all are striving for a common goal."

"Oh, Fanny," said Gervase Siddall, "do you really swallow all that Fourieristic hogwash about the seas turning to lemonade and tigers becoming tame? Hippopotami becoming beasts of burden?"

"Once the earth," said Fanny seriously, "is in harmony with the other planets and supplies her share of beneficial aroma, ceases to exhale the present pestilential vapors, then the climate of the earth will become temperate, vicious animals will be tame—"

Colin suppressed a smile.

"Oh yes, tell us about the anti-tigers," he said, leaning forward.

"Oh," Fanny said earnestly, "they will be a third again as big as tigers are now and able to carry seven travelers at once on their backs at a rate of twenty miles per hour!"

The next day, Colin and Florilla searched for the *Arethusa bulbosa*. They had left all of Woodland Place sleeping, except for Miss Potts just returning, somewhat dispirited, from another unsuccessful bat hunt. Since Woodland Place was near the edge of the Pines, they had to go quite far into the woods, canoeing from stream to stream till they reached the bogs preferred by the *arethusa*. They pulled the canoe up onto a grassy hummock and waded through knee deep marsh grass, till suddenly among the shades of green were splashes of magenta: a colony of *arethusa* in full bloom.

"There," Colin breathed, "in perfect bloom. Come on!"

Arethusa, Florilla reflected, must be named for the girl who became a Sicilian spring when the river god, Alpheus, pursued her.

Colin had his glass out and was gazing through it at the lens.

"Florrie," he called impatiently, "whatever are you about? You must come look at them. You can see why the common name is 'dragon's mouth.'"

"I like *arethusa*," Florilla said stubbornly. "I like the story."

"Oh. Well, all right. But at least come and look and bring me the notebook, will you?"

Florilla picked up the notebook and riffled through the pages, marking the entries in Colin's careful, italic hand. Slowly, she got up and made her way toward him, cramming the straw hat that usually hung down her back tightly on her head, to hide her face. She dropped the book beside him.

"I say, look out!" he cried. "You almost dropped it right on an orchid."

"There are plenty of them," Florilla said.

Colin looked at her oddly.

"Here," he said, handing her the glass. "Do look."

The *arethusas* were even more beautiful seen close up, like crested birds poised for flight. Taking the glass, she inspected the lolling dragon's tongue, pale pinkish white with streaks of magenta. How wonderful to be an orchid, to be discovered and so closely regarded.

"Isn't it incredible, Florrie? We have nothing like this in England."

"Yes," said Florilla softly.

She did get tired of some of the orchids, with their pale greeny-white flowers, much like leaves in color and shape, but these were glorious.

"I'm glad you're here," Colin said suddenly. "One just wants someone to talk to when one finds something like this. Someone to share it."

Florilla couldn't help herself.

"You could have brought Fanny."

"Fanny?"

"Fanny Greenough."

Colin looked perplexed.

"Why ever," he said, "would I want to do that?"

"So, she could share the *arethusa* with you."

"She doesn't care about orchids! Her head is full of Fourier's nonsense. She hasn't come with me to find all the others. I doubt that she can paddle a canoe. She certainly doesn't know these woods." He laughed. "She'd be no use to me. Chattering about pestilential vapors and the harmony of the spheres—not to mention anti-tigers."

Florilla sat, staring down at the *arethusa*, the straw hat shadowing her face so that he couldn't see her smile.

"You're my companion, Florrie," he said quietly. "I only dance with her."

They arrived home in time for tea, which was set out on the terrace each afternoon. Rosabel, her mouth stuffed with cake, was hanging from the huge trunk of a wisteria vine by both hands. Lady Amberwell, in a drift of muslin, was pouring tea. Florilla's hat hung down her back, and she was, as usual, sweaty and streaked with dirt.

"My dear," Lady Amberwell said, "that beautiful skin. You *must* wear your hat in the sun."

Most of the house party had left. The carriages had just taken Lord Amberwell and the other Philadelphians to the Camden ferry. Behind the huge silver teapot, Fanny, in plaid gingham sashed with blue, curls tied back, looked cool and composed. Florilla's dress clung to her back and legs, and her hair was pulled into a childish braid from which wisps escaped to stick to her flushed face.

"You look a sight, Florrie," Rosabel said after swallowing the cake. "I didn't know orchids were so dirty."

"Don't be pert," said her mother.

"Colin looks just as bad," Julian said mildly.

Colin's clothes were mud-spotted, his hair curled wildly round his ears and lay plastered against his forehead.

"We'll take a swim," he said. "Come on, Flora."

The women who came to Woodland Place were mainly wives or daughters. Aside from Euphemia Potts, the great exception was Marianna Fleming, who, as a celebrated bluestocking, went everywhere in her own right. She arrived late one night in a hired carriage, almost colliding with Euphemia Potts setting out on a bat hunt.

She descended coolly from the carriage, paid the driver, and was directing the disposition of her several boxes when Lady Amberwell appeared, surprisingly flustered, on the steps. She was dressed as Ceres because there was a *tableau vivant* in progress in the drawing room.

"My dear," Marianna Fleming said, holding her at arm's length and surveying the white gown caught up with gold, "how charming you look, and how in keeping with the house."

She herself, in a man's straw hat, bloomers, and a shirt of striped silk, heavily sashed at the waist, strongly resembled a character in a comic opera.

"Did my letter arrive?"

"I don't think so," Lady Amberwell said vaguely, "but we have been expecting you this month."

"Ah, good," said Mariana Fleming, "and may I hope to have my favorite room at the end of the hall? It was so quiet for writing."

"Of course," said Lady Amberwell.

Marianna Fleming was a scholar, critic, and essayist. She had sufficient money to do what she liked, and what she liked was to make her
way about hobnobbing with the important thinkers of her times. She was
an older cousin of Lady Amberwell, and she, too, remembered childhood visits to Alice Furnace and Woodland Place. This gave her a pro-
prietary attitude toward the house and most of the people in it. She still
came often since she lived in New York, where she kept a modest salon.
She smoked cigarillos after dinner and insisted on wearing variations of
her bloomer costume, including one in black velvet for evening.

"The female body," she said, "needs its freedom."

She was horrified to discover that Florilla tramped through woods and
marsh in a dress, and at once ordered Lady Amberwell's seamstress to run
up a costume like her own. Florilla found it a great deal more comfortable.

"Who is the child?" she asked Lady Amberwell.

Lady Amberwell related again the story of Florilla's arrival.

"How odd," said Marianna Fleming, "but how interesting. You say
she knows Latin and Greek."

That evening, Marianna Fleming addressed Florilla in Greek at dinner. Florilla answered without hesitation.

"Very good, my dear," said Marianna Fleming. "I can see that you
have been carefully taught."

After that, she took a great interest in Florilla, insisting that they read
Latin and Greek together in the evenings. She was also curious about
Florilla's psychic abilities, which she deduced from an evening of whist.

Marianna Fleming blew a cloud of smoke from her cigarillo.

"Have you ever done table tapping?"

Florilla shook her head.

"I'm sure you could, you know. Imagine it—imagine calling up Homer
or Shakespeare."

"Isn't it usually used," said Colin, "to get in touch with Great-Aunt So-and-So?"

"Pish," said Marianna Fleming scornfully. "One wants to speak to the great, the noble minds."

"What I think you are," said Colin to Florilla, "is a healer. When I hurt my leg, you took the pain away."

"Sometimes I can do that."

"How marvelous," said Marianna Fleming. "I have chronic trouble with my back. Perhaps you could help that."

And she immediately lay down flat on the floor, continuing to talk as Florilla knelt beside her:

"I have been at several seances in New York. Nothing of great interest, people's departed spouses and whatnot. However, I am convinced that the problem was with the medium. Mostly vulgar and uneducated persons, like those Fox sisters on their farm upstate. What do they know of Petrarch?"

"Concentrate," Florilla said. "Try to empty your mind."

"My dear child," Marianna Fleming said, "that would be exceedingly difficult, but my back does feel better."

Not long afterward, looking for *Platanthera nivea*, the snowy orchid, Colin and Florilla were caught in the open when a thunderstorm broke overhead. The day had been heavy and humid, but the towering dark clouds rose suddenly on the horizon. Florilla saw the first white streak of lightning. The clap of thunder came almost immediately. A sudden swell of wind shook the snowdrop blossoms of the orchids. Colin leaned protectively over them, lest the wind scatter the fragile flowerets of his perfect specimen. He got it into the press as the green storm light engulfed them and the first huge drops of rain began to fall. The sky was torn by jagged lightning. They were on a hummocky island in the midst of marshland, slashes of light eerily reflected in flat standing pools of water.

"We should stay here," Florilla yelled over the thunder. "It would be dangerous under the trees."

Colin stuffed the book and press into his bag. In the center of the hummock, they huddled together as the storm broke over them in blowing sheets of rain blurring everything but the dark outline of trees thrashing on the horizon. Florilla had seen summer storms like this before, had seen lightning split trees, start fires. Colin put his arms protectively around her. No weather he had ever seen had prepared him for this. It was at once terrifying and fascinating. Soaked to the skin, they clung to each other.

They were both dazed when the rain stopped, and a watery light spread round them.

"Flora," Colin said finally.

Florilla raised her head.

"I hope your notebook didn't get soaked," she said.

"Yes," Colin said, "I hope not." He was in fact appalled that he could have forgotten his entire summer's work while he held her. He scrambled up, discovering to his relief that the press had protected his book and the specimen snowy orchid.

"Luckily," he said, "the rain didn't keep up very long, or it would have soaked through."

They stood awkwardly.

"We'd better get back," Colin said with difficulty. "They're bound to be worried."

The storm had broken at Woodland Place. Lightning had, in fact, hit the weathervane on Freeman Jade's tower with a huge pop, which had caused him to look out just in time to see it shoot down the drainpipe and dig a huge furrow in the ground. Since then, he had been cowering in the library drinking China tea.

There had been much worry over Colin and Florilla, and they were sent to change while more tea and cakes were brought. Coming downstairs at different times, they sat on opposite sides of the tea table. Suddenly aware of each other, they jumped and excused themselves if their feet touched or their hands met over the plate of cakes. The parrots, loose in the room, had been impressed by the popping of lightning and startled everyone by imitating the sound perfectly.

12

It was late August; orchid hunting was coming to an end. They sought now the late flowering ladies' tresses and the autumn coral root. The names were things from fairy tales, and to Florilla the days became episodes of fancy: "Bring me the flower that blooms in the valley for half a day every hundred years."

They always gathered the scientific data first, then picnicked in the ferny depths of thickets, on the banks of ponds and streams, on grassy hummocks. There would be the smell of pines, of crushed fern, and the muddy smell of moss and rotting logs. The air would be full of the shrilling voice of crickets.

"I dread to announce," Lady Amberwell said at dinner, "that we are soon to receive a visit from that prying German woman who is on a tour of American manners and institutions."

"Miss Muehlberg," said Freeman Jade, "oh dear. A lady of strong convictions."

"She is bringing with her," Lady Amberwell continued, pushing away a parrot to choose a peach from the fruit bowl, "a young scientist who is interested in the explosive properties of the dust from the spores of club moss."

"Is he a botanist?" Colin asked.

"Some sort of engineer, I think. Thank heavens they'll be gone before Amberwell gets back. She drives him mad."

Irmgard Muehlberg arrived the next week. The carriage was dispatched to collect her from the North American Phalanx at Red Bank where she had been visiting friends still living in their cabins. She was a large, toothy woman, dressed in a brown satin dress with a tight basque, a plumed bonnet wedged on her head. She looked oddly out of place, but Florilla realized that this was because she had become so used to the theatrical costumes of Lady Amberwell and the others. The young man she had brought with her spoke no English. He was bony of figure and baleful of face, with fishy blue eyes and a limp, damp handshake. Irmgard Muehlberg's handshake was painfully strong. As well as a trunk of clothes, she had brought a second full of manuscripts.

"I must write about America," she would cry by way of explanation. "I must make it understood in the Old World."

She had been touring New England, she said, that first night at dinner, touring the mill towns. She had particularly spent time in Lowell, Massachusetts, but she had also been to the smaller towns, among them Franklinville, also in Massachusetts. She was very impressed by the Yankee girls, by their industry, their resourcefulness, their questioning spirits, and their love of learning.

"In the mills," she said, "they work from five in the morning till seven at night, and then they go to the lyceums to listen to lectures on Shakespeare, classical literature, or on foolish things like mesmerism and spiritualism and phrenology—my Fritz believes in that—also the health. The health, such a big interest in America: the water cure, Dr. Graham's diet. Everything new they want to know."

Here she dipped a large piece of bread in gravy and chewed loudly.

"You know, I think, for those girls this work is the only chance. Otherwise, it is, you know, the farm, the toil of the land forever. But you see they are not the riffraff, but the daughters of honest men. So, the manufacturers must create a decent society for them. It is planned, you see. It does not just happen as in England and other countries. There it is terrible."

She sighed.

"But I fear it is changing here. So many Irish now in Lowell, living in shanty towns and working for less pay. In a few years all will be changed. The manufacturers will take advantage. Sadly so."

Whereupon she helped herself liberally to the platter of meat as it was passed again.

"It is the hunger of the traveler," she said.

She seemed to be eating for two as Fritz took only vegetables and toyed with them gloomily.

"I am very interested," she continued, "in the structure of institutions and communities in the New World. I am visiting Brook Farm, but that is now—pouf!—gone. Mr. Alcott remains in Concord with his theories. As you know, the North American Phalanx at Red Bank is diminished. Many have left. Only a few old friends remain. It was sad to visit them."

"These utopian communities," said Freeman Jade, "seem to be short-lived."

"Theories," she replied practically, "are useless without bread."

Fritz, on her right hand, said something to her in German.

"Ah, yes," she said, "there is a place near here—or not very far—that I would like to visit very much. It is called Benderville."

At this point, Florilla, who had been listening with some interest, almost dropped the spoon she was holding.

"It is very interesting," she continued, "a manufacturing town based largely on the theories of Robert Owen and built just here in the forest."

"Oh yes," said Lady Amberwell vaguely. "I have heard of it. It is quite a distance from us."

"No matter, dear lady," said Miss Muehlberg. "I shall go one day in your carriage. When I visited Franklinville in Massachusetts, I was told of it by the owner of mills there. Benderville is run by his brother."

Florilla was caught in a confusion of feeling, a homesickness for the old mansion, Ananda's grumbling, and Lethe's silent ways, for Benjamin Bender himself. She missed him. But even greater was the fear of discovery. What would he do if he knew where she was? Silly, she thought, there would be no reason that Miss Muehlberg would mention her.

Fritz spent all day in the woods gathering foxtail club moss. One early morning, he was netted by Euphemia Potts who took him for an antipodal bat or the Jersey Devil. Fritz was furious; she was disappointed.

Miss Muehlberg got on everyone's nerves, especially Marianna Fleming's.

"I hope," she said, "that woman isn't trying to write anything *subtle* about America."

"I think she describes what she sees," said Lady Amberwell mildly. She was watching Florilla and Colin, who were laughing over a game of backgammon. Something struck her. She thought she should have noticed it before. She began to watch them more closely, the way they bent their heads together at dinner, the laughter that sometimes came from the summerhouse in the evening. She called herself a fool for not foreseeing something like this.

"I hope things aren't getting serious," she said to Marianna Fleming.

"So do I. The girl's mind is far too good to waste on marriage."

"Well," said Lady Amberwell, "that wasn't exactly what I was thinking."

"Then what *were* you thinking?"

"The expectations for Colin."

"A very clever, charming boy. A bit of a fanatic, but then that is often charming in itself."

"The thing is," said Lady Amberwell, "that he is engaged to be married to an English heiress."

"An arranged marriage? Surely not."

Lady Amberwell gave an impatient shrug.

"You know Amberwell's late sister was Colin's mother, his father is Lord Fenhope, and Colin is the heir to the title, a large estate, and a beautiful house, Amaryllis Court, all of which, I regret to say, is in danger of being lost if there is no infusion of money.

"Is Colin a party to this?"

"Of course. Amberwell said he never seemed to mind whom he married. He loves the place and sees that the money is needed. He wants desperately to keep the rather extensive greenhouses and the gardens established by his grandfather, also a botanist. To keep those and do his field trips—which cost a certain amount—are his main concerns. Or were. He didn't seem to be very interested in romantic love."

"Well," said Marianna Fleming, "in that case, it is very wrong of him to trifle with the feelings of so young a girl. I shall tell him so tonight."

"Now, Marianna," said Lady Amberwell soothingly, "let's not be headlong. He is leaving soon for his southern field trip. I think that would be the time to talk to the girl."

"The *girl*? Why don't you talk to *him*?"

Lady Amberwell sighed.

"Women," she said, "are often better able to see sense."

13

With the coming of September, Florilla was haunted by the thought that Colin would be leaving, if only for a few weeks. She had begun tutoring the children, which she did enjoy. With no set plan to follow, she just made up the lessons as she went along. They read whatever books she chose from the library downstairs, a collection that was not much smaller than Benjamin Bender's. She was glad that she would have something to fill up the time while Colin was gone.

"I'm leaving my New Jersey specimens here," Colin told her on a late September afternoon, "in the cupboard in my room. If there's a fire or a flood, I'd like you to save them."

Florilla nodded, trying not to laugh.

In the tower room, Freeman Jade had a basket and a rope which he planned to use to lower his manuscript in case of fire. Being high up, he was less worried about floods.

Colin checked his books and his notes twenty times. He almost forgot to pack any clothes.

"I'll be back at the end of November," he said to Florilla, "and then we will go looking for *Schizaea pusilla*. By then the ground cover should have died down enough to make it easier to find. Meanwhile, if you could find me the *Habenaria integra*—it's the only one I haven't got."

Again, Florilla nodded.

The carriage was at the door to take him to Atsion, where he would catch the Tuckerton stage to Camden, thence by ferry and road to Philadelphia where Lord Amberwell had arranged for his travel south. Florilla was to go with him to Atsion to see him off.

Atsion was a bog iron town that, like Alice Furnace, had fallen on hard times. The main street of the town passed by the Greek Revival mansion built by the first of the iron masters. A little shabby, it was still imposing. They passed a church, stopping at the general store where the stage would halt.

"I wish you were coming with me," Colin said, frowning. "I'm so used to having your help."

"You'll have other botanists."

He continued to frown.

"They're usually," he said, "more hindrance than help. Always wanting to be the *first* to see anything."

He paused.

"But more than that, I'll just miss you."

He took her hand.

A swirl of dust in the distance announced the arrival of the stage, its four horses going at a brisk trot. Pulling up, the driver got down and took Colin's luggage to stow in the back. A boy came running with buckets to water the horses. No other passengers were waiting, but Florilla could see several in the coach. Colin kissed her quickly on the cheek, turned, and climbed in. He leaned out of the window.

"You will find me the *habenaria*?" he asked anxiously, the intensity in his face equal to the strongest declaration of principle—or love.

Florilla sighed

"Yes," she said, "I'll try."

Finally, the driver remounted, and with a crack of the long whip, the stage set off, the horses once again trotting smartly. Florilla watched it out of sight.

The carriage swayed through the woods on the way back to Woodland Place. Florilla, sitting alone on the tufted plush seat, realized that with Colin's leaving some screen had dropped away, and there was nothing between her and the daily business of living. Memories of Benderville came back to her. She thought about Benjamin Bender. She would have liked to let him know where she was, but it was geographically too close and otherwise too precarious. She was afraid that she could be snatched away, that she owed him too much not to return if asked, that if anyone at Benderville knew where she was, her father would find out.

As the coachman drove at a steady pace along the lonely roads, she began to fear meeting Munion. However, they passed no one, and by the time they reached Woodland Place, she had wrapped herself securely in her memories of Colin.

Lady Amberwell saw this and decided it was time to break her news. She went to find Boffin, who had by now painted his way to the last figure of his mural, Daphne turning into a blossoming laurel, the one for which he wanted Florilla to pose.

"Boffin," she said, "what are we to do?

"Do?" Boffin replied absently.

"Flora and Colin."

"Charming," said Boffin. "They go together very well. I'm sure I'll get *Going West* into the Royal Academy show."

"Be serious, Boffin. "You know he is to marry Sophronia Scrubdale."

"Ah yes, heiress to the Yorkshire woolen mills?"

"Yes," said Lady Amberwell impatiently, it is the only way to save Amaryllis Court."

Boffin stepped back to gaze critically at his rendering of bog asphodel.

"Now that is a place worth saving."

"Well, of course. But how do I tell our wood nymph?"

"Let me try," Boffin said.

Florilla, as Daphne, held her pose, draped in green and clutching two branches of laurel. Boffin, up on a ladder, hummed as he sketched on the wall.

"Did you know," he said, "that Colin will one day become Lord Fenhope? And one day soon, probably, because his father is really quite old?"

Florilla, trying to hold Daphne's expression of desperation, did not reply.

"Yes," Boffin went on, "he has this great pile of a house in Oxfordshire. Beautiful place. Makes this house look like a cottage. Falling down, though. Some old fool lost the fortune gambling at the end of the last century. Hold your arm up a little higher, that's good. And Colin has to find some way to keep it going or sell it."

For a few moments Boffin sketched furiously.

"Botany just won't do it," he said. "Don't you see? No money in botany."

Florilla did not see, though Boffin thought he had made himself abundantly clear. She found the information about Colin interesting, as all information about Colin was interesting, but she didn't relate any of it to herself.

Lady Amberwell, however, made it plain several nights later as they strolled in the rose garden gathering the late roses.

"Flora," she said, "there is something I must tell you though I am dreadfully afraid it will make you unhappy."

Florilla's heart skipped.

"Is it my teaching?"

"No, no. That has been entirely satisfactory. It is about Colin."

Florilla turned pale.

"Is he all right? I—"

"Quite all right," Lady Amberwell interrupted, "this is something about his future."

As she explained the situation of Amaryllis Court, Florilla recognized Boffin's attempt.

"That means, my dear," Lady Amberwell finished, "that while I know you two are very fond of each other, I wanted to warn you about going beyond friendship. You are very young, and it is very easy at your age to make proximity into romance. I wanted to make it clear that there is no real future in it for you."

"He never told me," Florilla said slowly. "He never told me about her."

To her dismay, Lady Amberwell saw that things had indeed gone farther than she had hoped.

Florilla found herself plunged into a misery so total that her qualms of conscience about Benderville, her fears of the reappearance of Munion became mere pinpricks. She wasn't sure that she had ever really thought about marrying Colin, but the idea that he would be taken from her, shut away with someone else forever, was a terrible one. Behind every word she said, or that was said to her, ran the thought that Colin would be gone forever. She wondered what she had supposed would happen. She knew that he would go back to England eventually, in a year's time in fact, and that much of that year would be spent, not at Woodland Place, but on plant hunting trips. The answer was that she hadn't thought at all. She had assumed that if he cared for her, she wouldn't lose him. Yet he was engaged to someone else and had never told her. This added humiliation to pain. Florilla, who had managed often on her own, who had an education, had worked for a living, had nonetheless fallen prey to that demon, romantic love. That was what Mariana Fleming told her.

"Women," she said as they sat by themselves in the library after time spent reading Latin, something from which Florilla derived pleasure and relief, "must have lives of their own. I have never married, and I am thirty-five. You must think of the future. You have a good basic education. You could go on, go to university."

"Oxford doesn't take women," Florilla said.

"Not *Oxford*! But there is a college in this country that takes women, Oberlin in Ohio. There are also many teaching jobs to be had in the West, in all those mission schools."

Marianna Fleming felt that she was counseling Florilla to choose an independence like her own. She failed, however, to consider that her independence was supported by a considerable income.

Alone in her room at night, Florilla thought of running away. Running away was natural to her and so far in her life had turned out very well. She had run away from Sim Place to Benderville and from Benderville to Woodland Place. She sat on the swan bed asking herself if she could flee now, flee from the certainty of seeing Colin again. But where would she go? Not back to Benderville. She could, she supposed, go to Philadelphia to find work. She had her wages to start out with, but she knew nothing of cities. The decision was too enormous. Numbly, she thought she would just go on until she could decide what to do. She didn't want to be foolish. There was only one thing that she knew she wanted: to find the *Habenaria integra* for Colin.

At night she dreamed of Colin, and always they were hunting a mysterious orchid, an orchid without a name. In one of those dreams, she had lost him and was alone in the woods near Sim Place. There she saw blooming not the orchid they sought, but the pale-yellow flowers she remembered. Waking with a start, she realized that those were the flowers of *Habenaria integra*, the specimen Colin had begged her to find. Florilla was too excited to go back to sleep. She lay there calculating how long it would take her to get to Sim Place by canoe. When the breakfast bell rang, she raced downstairs, filled with purpose for the first time since Lady Amberwell's confidences.

Her animation was noted at breakfast. Lady Amberwell thought that young hearts mended quickly. Marianna Fleming thought that Florilla had given up the heart for the mind. Boffin hoped that she was falling in love with him. Miss Muehlberg, spreading marmalade thickly on her toast, noticed nothing. She had received an invitation to visit that fine social experiment, Benderville.

14

On Wednesdays, the children had no lessons. That week, as Frau Muehlberg whirled off in the carriage to Benderville, Florilla set out for Sim Place. She carried her own notebook and Colin's flower press.

The late September sun was warm, though the shadows, as she paddled the twisting streams, were cold. When she had gone as far as she could on the water, she pulled the canoe up on land, hiding it carefully in a thicket. She knew that she was in dangerous territory. She told herself that she could avoid the shanty and that, in any case, it had been empty so long that it was doubtful her father came there. She ran down the familiar paths till she came to the remembered grassy clearing. There they were, a large clump of *Habenaria integra*, bobbing in the light afternoon breeze. Though the season was late, there were several spears of perfect bloom. Breathless, she knelt beside them. Choosing the best, she had plucked them carefully and set them in her basket when she was aware of footsteps on the path behind her. Jumping up, she spun around. There stood Jack Munion.

"Well, well," he said, "come to gather a posy for your old father?"

"The old man told me you'd run off," Munion said.

Outside it was still bright afternoon, but inside the shack it was dark. Chinks of light from the flimsy walls and the boarded-over windows were enough to show Florilla the familiar shapes of the room: the wood stove, the rocker her grandmother had favored, the rickety table with its two chairs. There were even cups and plates on the table, where she had set them for breakfast the day her grandmother died.

Munion grinned at her.

"Don't the place look just the same," he said.

She stood by the stove, holding herself as though there might be a chance to run, but he had locked the door, and there was no way out.

"Your poor father," he said, "didn't think he'd ever see you again in this world. Just run off like that into the blue. The old man was pretty cut up about it. Didn't think you'd do something like that." He grinned again. "Guess you're more a Munion than anyone wants to think. That's what I always said."

Florilla glared at him. She couldn't see his face very well in the dimness, only his cocky stance, legs apart, arms folded over his chest.

"What were you doing?" he said. "Where you been anyway? You gonna tell me?"

Florilla shook her head.

"Just loose in the woods? Running around picking flowers?"

"I'm not going to tell you."

"You've been somewhere. That costume you're wearing. You didn't get that at Benderville. No lady wears anything like that. Why those are as good as trousers. And I'd give to know what you got in this thing."

Picking up the basket, Munion dumped its contents onto the floor. The flower press landed with a bang and the spikes of *habenaria* tumbled around it, seeming to glow with a pale-yellow phosphorescence.

"No!" Florilla cried and sprang forward to gather them up.

Munion laughed.

"Valuable are they? I seen them flowers grow summers before. Never knew they were worth anything."

Florilla had gathered them carefully. The perfect bloom was unscathed.

"Oh please," she said, "please let me put them in the press."

Munion said nothing, watched her as though she were a lunatic as she carefully unscrewed the press, laid the flowers in and screwed it tight again. She felt as though she had been given one last wish, redeemed a final task. She didn't ask herself how she would ever get them to Colin.

Munion sat down and put his heavy booted feet up on the table.

"Sit down," he said. "You've got your flowers. I want to talk to you."

Florilla stayed where she was. He reached over and shoved the rocker toward her.

"Sit down, girl," he said. He didn't raise his voice and continued to smile. "You better get used to doing what I tell you. I ain't going to say it twice."

Florilla stared at him. A slat of light from the boarded window caught his bright blonde hair. His eyes glittered coldly; she didn't have to see their icy blue color.

"I said sit down."

"No," Florilla said.

He sprang from his chair before she could move and flung her into the rocker. He stood over her, grabbing the arms of the chair before she could get her balance.

"You ought to do what I tell you the first time," he said mildly. "You just ain't used to obeying your father, running around all over the place the way you do."

He stood over her, arms folded.

"I want to know where you been," he said. "It's been four months now since you ran out on Bender. I want to know what you been up to, what all this fancyin' around with wildflowers is about."

"I won't tell you," Florilla said.

"You will," he replied, "in time. And we got plenty of that."

"What are you going to do with me?"

"*Do* with you? I ain't going to *do* nothing with you. You're going to help your poor old father earn his living. You stay here. I'll get us some food from the wagon."

He went out the door, locking it behind him.

Florilla leapt to her feet. She shoved open the door to the bedroom. In the draft, a cloud of feathers rose and drifted slowly down in the dull light from cracks in the boarded windows. To her horror, Florilla saw that the room was exactly as she had left it on the day that she and Dr. Still had buried her grandmother. The covers were thrown back on the bed, and the tumbled pillows had been torn by wintering squirrels. On the wall, her grandmother's bonnet and cloak hung next to her own brown calico dress. She took it down, a child's dress faded and mended. Holding it, she could see herself as the child she had been on the day that Dr. Peace had taken her to Benderville. She sat down on the bed, and it seemed that no time had passed, that she had never been to Benderville at all. The power of the old woman the Pines had called a witch seemed to rise up and claim her being. She heard her voice, old and thin.

"Third generation. That's what you are, child."

Frau Muehlberg had been shown all over Benderville. She found it interesting in its similarity to, and difference from, the New England mill towns. She was particularly interested in Benjamin Bender's theories on education. She questioned him and Mr. Magreavey in great detail about the Benderville school. Although much was done for the children at an early age, it surprised her that there were no lyceums, no further education for workers once they had left the school. Since so many of Benderville's workers were women, she asked particular questions about their education.

"I have not found," Benjamin Bender said, "the further education of women to be worthwhile."

Frau Muehlberg was shocked. This was not the attitude of the northern mill owners who told her earnestly that the life of the mills provided an education for girls who would otherwise have had no more than a few years in a rural school. They had, at times, made the work in the mills seem incidental to the gift of an education.

"In the towns I visited," she began, "in Lowell and in Franklinville, the mill owners did not feel that way."

"But what did they provide? Evening lectures? Bible classes? Scraps of philosophy taught by a dabbling minister? Perhaps group classes in Latin or Greek or German taught by someone the girls themselves hired? That is just a smattering. It is useless for women to pursue a true classical education."

"Why is that, Mr. Bender?"

Benjamin Bender rubbed his forehead. He had just seen Florilla so clearly, the golden head bent over her books, and the pain the vision brought was as sharp as ever. He sighed.

"They don't go on," he said wearily. "They don't stick to it. They just get married," he paused, "or whatever. It's like teaching a dog to walk on its hind legs. The dog may be capable of it, but where is the point?"

"Or," he muttered under his breath, "a fish to sing opera."

"Ah," said Frau Muehlberg, "that is not always so. I have met a most intelligent girl, beautiful with golden hair, but reading Latin and Greek. She has come, none knows how, to Woodland Place."

Benjamin Bender stared at her across the tea table, which had been set out on the veranda in the shade of the wisteria vines. Could this foreign woman, black bombazine stretched taut over her large frame, this woman who was now eating a huge slice of cake, be talking about Florilla? His hand trembled as he poured himself another cup of tea and asked the girl's name.

"Flora it is," said Frau Muehlberg, spreading jam on her cake. "Flora like the goddess of spring and flowers. And, one day, like a goddess, she appeared out of the wood."

"Will she stay at Woodland Place?"

"But of course. She is to be governess to the children. Lady Amberwell loves her as though she were her own daughter. After all, she is beautiful—when one is young and beautiful and clever, it is easy to be loved."

Yes, thought Benjamin Bender. He had loved her. Andrew McKenzie had loved her. Since Florilla had run away, the dye master had become almost reclusive, making excuses to work longer hours, experimenting with new dyes. He spent hours in the woods collecting mosses, lichen and autumn's ripening fruits and berries. Late into the night, the fire burned in one of the small stoves as he boiled together the heads of flowers, berries, stalks, leaves and moss, dyed strands of roving which he hung, numbered, on a board. He did it to replace her because he couldn't forget. And yet, Benjamin Bender knew that he would not call her back. She had found a place in the world beyond the mill where her father would be unlikely to find her.

"Frau Muehlberg," he said, "would you take a letter from me to the girl you mention. I am interested in how she acquired her education."

"The education of the women," said Frau Muehlberg, "is of very great importance. It is through the women that the values of this new society can be transmitted."

Benjamin Bender excused himself, went into the library, took a sheet of paper and began to write.

Jack Munion shoved chunk wood in the stove and lit it.

"Here," he said, dumping the contents of a sack on the table. Make dinner."

"Go on," he added, "don't just stand there looking. Do it."

"I don't know how to cook."

"Well, I guess you can fry bacon all right."

Florilla moved to the shelves by the stove and took down the iron frying pan. It was rusted, filled with cobwebs and mouse droppings.

"I'll have to wash it," Florilla said.

Jack Munion laughed.

"Think I'm going to tell you to take out and wash it under the pump, do you? Not sharp enough. Give it here."

He grabbed it from her and went out, turning the key in the lock. Florilla began to cut the greasy slab of bacon.

"I am disappointed not to find her," Frau Muehlberg complained at dinner at Woodland Place. "I have brought back a letter for her."

She was rather annoyed that her very particular descriptions of Benderville had met with a preoccupied audience.

"A letter? For Flora?"

"From Mr. Bender. He said he is interested in how she acquired her education."

"Really," murmured Lady Amberwell.

Night fell. Lanterns were hung on the veranda and at the end of the dock. Search parties had been sent out in canoes and had returned empty-handed. Lady Amberwell and Marianna Fleming sat by the drawing room windows, looking out into the night, clear under a full moon.

"If she were on her way home now," Lady Amberwell said, "she would be able to find her way. It's very bright."

"You don't suppose she could have run away again? You say you think she was running away when she came to you first?"

"It seemed that way. But why would she run away from us?"

"Didn't you tell her all that nonsense about Amaryllis Court and what's her name, the wool merchant's daughter?"

"Sophronia Scrubdale. Well, yes."

"Mightn't that be enough to make her run away?"

Early the next morning, a search party went out again. They canoed down the rivers and through the spongs, they canoed right past the place where Florilla had pulled her canoe up on the bank. They saw nothing because Jack Munion, by the light of the moon, had hauled it up into the undergrowth and hidden it completely.

Jack Munion kept Florilla locked in the shack. He was gone with the caravan most days, making himself visible in the nearby towns to ensure that Florilla's disappearance would not be connected with him. He even went to Benderville early one morning, arriving at the mansion just as Benjamin Bender was setting out for his morning visit to the mill.

"Good morning, sir," said Jack Munion. "I've come to inquire after my daughter."

Benjamin Bender looked narrowly at the man.

"She's gone, Munion," he said finally. "She ran away."

Jack Munion frowned.

"Ran away? When was that?"

"In late spring."

"I don't believe you."

Benjamin Bender shrugged.

"It's the truth."

"You know where she is?"

And one day, like a goddess, she appeared out of the wood. He heard Frau Muehlberg's words in his head, but he said:

"I have no idea. There's been no word."

"That's a pity then," said Jack Munion. "She could be dead."

"Well, if she's dead, she's of no interest to you. She can't increase your income if she's dead."

Jack Munion narrowed his eyes.

"If you'd let me take her when I came," he said quietly, "she'd be with me now. Whatever you did to her, you made her unhappy and she ran away."

He waved one hand in the air and a ribbon of silk scarves cascaded over his head, a quivering silken rainbow that fell between his feet. He passed his hands over them and paper flowers grew, yellow, blue and red.

"That's where she belonged, Mr. Bender," he said, "with me in my trade. My Florilla wasn't made to be shut up in a mill."

"I didn't shut her up in the mill, Munion."

Jack Munion shrugged. He pulled another flower from behind his ear and smiled.

"Whatever you did," he said, "was wrong. Good day, Mr. Bender."

He smiled and drove away quite pleased with himself.

At first, when Munion left in the mornings, Florilla would run round the shack like a trapped bird, pushing at the boarded windows, shaking the locked door. Then she would sink back onto a chair, comforted by the thought that the plan was ridiculous. How could he hold her by force, expect to make her work? She would stand on the stage and do nothing. She would destroy his act. But as the days passed, she began to see things differently. He planned to leave the Pines, even the state. He had told her so. And perhaps that suited her. She would run away again, but somewhere a long way from these woods. Benderville was behind her, even that part of her childhood that was trapped in this house was behind her, and so were the days at Woodland Place. The future stretched ahead of her without mark or feature. Munion had given an awful sort of form to the emptiness.

Florilla took care of the animals, the doves, the rabbit, and the black hen that Munion brought inside in their cages. She let them out and they hopped and flew around the shack while she carefully described the *habenaria* in her notebook.

"I been to see the old man at Benderville," Munion said as Florilla silently cleared away supper. "He was all upset about you running off, not knowing where you were.

"You ain't much company," he grumbled when Florilla didn't respond. He leaned forward on his elbows.

"You can keep the manners," he snarled, "but everything else you learned about being a fine lady, you better forget. You're in my world now."

New England

Autumn/Winter 1855-1856

15

They left Sim Place in the middle of the night. Munion woke her roughly and bundled her into the wagon. He tied her hand and foot because he still didn't trust her not to run away.

Florilla remembered the caravan. There was a door on one side and a high window at the back, open for light and ventilation. Munion had built it himself with two bunk beds and shelves designed to hold the caged animals and all the other props of the magician's trade. Another hinged shelf folded out from the wall making a table. Beside it was a narrow built-in dresser, tin plates and cups held by a plate rail, the drawers beneath filled with scarves and flags, artificial flowers and strings of glass beads.

Though she knew her father to be a fraud, Florilla still felt the familiar magic in the things themselves, the rainbow colors, the iridescent silk, the gentle doves, the black rabbit, even in the bit of mirror on the wall, positioned so that it reflected the stars in the small square of the back window and the wavering arcs of lantern light.

They drove for several hours. The ropes, though loosely tied, made her hands and feet numb. She watched the sky lighten in the mirror till the sun was high overhead. She remembered the last time she had been in this wagon. It had been at Sea Grove. Her father had come one day across the causeway to the island to see her and her mother. She remembered a spotted horse, unhitched, grazing in the dunes.

"Go in," he had said, lifting her up into the open doorway. "You used to live in it when we all traveled together."

She stroked the rabbit and touched cautiously the feathers of the doves, softer than anything she had ever felt, a jewel-colored, enchanted world. Then she heard him shouting, her mother's voice high and frightened. He came and lifted her roughly down, handing her to her mother, who was crying. Paradise had shattered around her, and she had begun to fear him.

She knew when they left the woods because she no longer smelled the pines and because the sand no longer muffled the sounds of the wheels and of the horse's hooves. She heard Munion shout to the horse, and their pace quickened. Sometimes they were passed by other wagons. She watched the window, saw the light become flatter, making her think they were near the sea. Once, in the middle of the day, he pulled the wagon off the road and got out bread and cheese for lunch.

"Where are we?" she asked. "Where are we going?"

"Up the coast," he said, "that's where we're going. That's all you need to know."

At evening, they reached Long Branch. They stayed in rooms over the livery stable, on one of the meaner streets behind the dazzling splendor of Ocean Avenue, which fronted the sea and was dominated by big hotels. It was clear that Munion had been here before because the ostler knew him, and there was an amount of laughing and banter. He had to untie Florilla to take her out of the wagon, gripping her firmly by the arm.

"I'm not going to run away," she said angrily. "Where would I run?"

"I ain't taking chances," Munion replied. He pushed her ahead of him through a door into a tack room, smelling of leather and the clean sweat of animals, and up a narrow, dark staircase into a loft. Munion let go of her arm, and she went straight to the only window. The loft was higher than most of the neighboring buildings. She could see every-thing: the carriages passing on Ocean Avenue, the boardwalk along the top of the sand bluffs, the sea glimmering toward an infinite horizon.

Munion came and stood behind her.

"See those big, fancy hotels? That's where I do my act. They know me there.

"You better do things right," he muttered, half to himself. "You do it right and there won't be no more staying in pokey rooms. We'll stay at the Mansion House."

He paused.

Though she still had her back to him, she sensed that he was looking at her.

"Clothes," he said. "I'll buy you clothes. And jewels."

"I don't want clothes," she said deliberately, "or jewels. But for now, I'll do what you want."

As she said the words, the sunset clouds on the sea's horizon seemed to move, to form themselves into the walls of something, and she imag-ined that she was seeing, across those leagues of water, the golden stones of Amaryllis Court as Colin had described it.

On his many visits, Jack Munion had made friends in Long Branch. He had begun with his wagon on Ocean Avenue, reading cards or palms or anything else anyone wanted. When it was seen that he was drawing considerable interest—for he was a deft magician—the manager of one of the hotels approached him about doing a show in the ballroom. He had done several with some success. The season was ending now, but they were happy enough to have him return.

"If it goes well," he told Florilla, "maybe we'll go on to Philadelphia."

For hours at stretch, Munion rehearsed her. At dawn they were up, working with cards, with objects in boxes.

"When they come up on stage," he said, "you *gotta* see what they want.

"I don't know what you mean. I might not see anything."

"You'll see it," he growled. "If they want to see their dear departed, you'll see 'em."

"You said it wouldn't be that," Florilla cried. "You said it would only be picking out cards."

"Don't you tell me," Munion said, pushing his face close to hers, "that you can't tell things about people just by looking at them. You've got the powers, I *know* that. Third generation. You got 'em straight from that great-grandmother witch you got."

"Witch?"

"Yes, witch. Folks thought she took the Jersey Devil for her lover. They hunted her down."

Suddenly, he reached out and grabbed Florilla's hair.

"You listen," he said, "I'm going to make you a witch, and then you'll have to stick with me. On your own, they'll do you in. You got powers, you need protection."

They stood by the window, and sunset was slowly staining the light. It flushed his face redder, angrier.

"And if they come wanting you to lay hands on 'em and heal them, you'll do that too."

"I'll heal," Florilla said sulkily. "There can't be any wrong in that."

"But you gotta do it right," he said, "you gotta put drama in it, make it seem like a trance."

"But it isn't a trance. That's like lying."

Munion leaned over her. For a moment she thought he would hit her, but he turned away, grinding his fists against his forehead.

"Oh, Lord," he moaned, "why couldn't it be me with the powers? I'd shine it up. I'd make it look so fine!"

"It's a pretty good audience for the end of the season," Munion said.

They were waiting behind a curtain as the opening act, a phrenologist, "read" his last subject, a young woman writhing with anxious giggles and with a head of curls that should have made the discerning of the geography of her skull exceptionally difficult.

"The bump of amativeness," he said with resonance, "seems to be highly developed in this subject."

Here the girl's silent giggles exploded in a sound like a whinny. She jumped with embarrassment, causing the phrenologist's white hands to flutter in the air. Florilla could see that sweat had plastered his own scanty hair to the knobby contours of his head. He released his anguished subject, and the audience clapped enthusiastically as the curtain was drawn across the stage. The phrenologist swabbed his forehead with a handkerchief.

"Come on," Munion hissed at Florilla, "we have to get this act up."

Mechanically, she helped him set up the tables and boxes. The phrenologist was pressed into service to move a gilt chair to the center of the stage for Florilla. He seemed to have nowhere particular to go and became a willing accomplice, carrying the dove cages, the juggling bats, the flags and flowers. He peered very curiously at Florilla.

"My dear," he said, "allow me to say that I perceive a large bump of mystery. I should like to read your skull.

Munion, overhearing, stopped.

"That's perfect," he said. "You can do that. In the act. After I've done a few tricks, you come out with me and tell them about her skull. Then we'll do the act. That'll get 'em. They won't think it's fake then."

When the curtain drew back, Munion was discovered alone. Watching him from behind the curtain, Florilla had to admire his showmanship. He drew himself up, seemed to expand so that he was no longer a stocky man in a stained costume but a mysterious gypsy whose sash glittered with sequins. His moves, quick and sinuous, were themselves hypnotic. The audience was completely silent as he created his illusory world, as doves flew out of dusters and the rabbit appeared from a bowl where apples had been. He drew from a silk scarf a bouquet of paper flowers, broke an egg and produced a chicken, the black hen who clucked and fussed on the table. Dramatically, he scooped her up, shoved her into one of the wooden cages. The audience clapped loudly, called for more, but he raised his hands and waited for silence. When it came, he spoke in his strange light voice with its cracked timbre.

"Ladies and gentlemen, I bring you something extraordinary. Professor Pargiter, who was with you earlier, will come forward to explain the phenomenon you are about to witness."

"Come along my dear," Dr. Pargiter whispered to Florilla and they stepped out from behind the curtain into the glare of lights.

The crowd seemed to Florilla to be one huge, hydra-headed beast, sighing and coughing.

"Ladies and gentlemen," Dr. Pargiter began. "I have spoken to you of the contours of the cranium, of the topography that reveals to us the virtues and vices of the subject. I have been given by Mr. Munion, the magician, the opportunity to show you how true a science is the science of phrenology by reading the head of his young assistant."

"Rosemalia," Munion hissed from behind the curtain.

Florilla was startled by her new name. She almost laughed.

"Miss Rosemalia," Dr. Pargiter said. "In this subject the organ of mystery is more highly developed than in any head that I have ever read. This is the head of one who has staggering psychic powers."

Munion stepped out from behind the curtain. The audience hushed and the *tableau* on the stage was, for a moment, frozen: Dr. Pargiter, his hands on Florilla's head; Munion smiling, standing slightly apart.

"And now," Munion spoke, his voice commanding for all its lightness, "I shall demonstrate the powers of the beautiful Rosemalia. Come here, my dear."

Florilla looked straight at him. Their eyes met. What, she wondered, would happen if she were to turn and run. She wavered. His eyes held hers. As though she had left her body, she saw herself running off the stage, into the streets of Long Branch, losing herself among the carriages and promenaders, running into the country, the woods, back to Woodland Place. Except that there was nothing to run to.

"Rosemalia," Munion said, "I am going to give this deck of cards to Dr. Pargiter. You will be blindfolded."

He stepped to the footlights and showed the audience the heavy black cloth blindfold. He approached Florilla. Again, she seemed to stand outside herself, but this time she was running down the main street of Benderville, although she didn't know if she was running toward the mansion or away from it. Munion tied the blindfold over her eyes, plunging her into darkness.

"Now, Rosemalia, he said, "the professor will hold a card up to the audience and you must concentrate and tell us what it is."

Florilla saw the card in her mind the way she had seen the cards playing whist at Woodland Place. She called out the number perfectly ten times. The audience drew in a collective breath.

Munion removed the blindfold and began to ask people up on stage to have Florilla guess things about them. She found it easy. He would ask her to tell them how many children they had, where they were born, where they lived. She could answer as surely as if those things were written on all those strange faces. She wondered that she had never noticed this gift before, perhaps because no one had ever asked it of her. It was simple enough and possibly useful.

When the girl came up on stage, she wasn't prepared for what she saw. She was searching the drawn, sallow face for trivial things. She saw illness, and, impulsively, reached out to touch her. She forgot the lights, forgot the people.

"Turn around," she said, standing behind the girl, hands on her shoulders. She could feel her own energy flowing through her fingers. She couldn't take her hands away although they tingled painfully. The girl gave several odd, jerking movements, then stood utterly still. Gradually, the tingling in Florilla's fingers lessened, ceased. She removed her hands. The girl remained still.

"Go," Florilla said gently, "you will be well."

She spoke in a strong, clear voice though she had forgotten completely about the audience.

The girl turned on her a drowned, bewildered look and stood entranced.

"Go on," Florilla said again, and the girl obeyed.

The audience was silent as she made her way back to her seat, uncertain of what it had witnessed. Then the whispering began. The sound, like wind in the trees, made it seem that she wandered the roads near Benderville in November, the lowering sun dazzling her eyes. Far away she heard Munion's voice and wondered vaguely if she were near the shack.

"Rosemalia," he was calling. "Rosemalia!"

And suddenly the trees dissolved, and she was back on the brightly lit stage. Dr. Pargiter was staring at her, and Munion was drawing her forward into the applause that broke like waves.

"You have seen it," he said. "You have seen Rosemalia's healing power. Come back tomorrow night."

After that, the second part of the act was healing. The magic and the card reading and a bit of phrenology by Dr. Pargiter, now part of the act, only led up to it. Munion was overjoyed: the summer season might be over, but there would always be interest in a healer. He had assurances from the manager of the hotel that they could continue through the fall. He was thinking about talking to some of the managers of other hotels. No end to the possibilities.

Only there was an end, and it came swiftly. On Sunday afternoons when there was no evening performance, Florilla was taken out walking either by Munion or Dr. Pargiter. On one such afternoon, they observed a carriage stopping at the hotel, a party of elegant people descended.

"Rich," Munion said happily. "Rich people come when they want, doesn't have to be high season."

But Florilla had stopped, and, pulling her scarf round her face, was staring at them.

"Know them do you?" Munion said, laughing.

"Yes," Florilla said, "I do."

She knew them as friends of Lord and Lady Amberwell who had often stayed at Woodland Place.

"Are you sure?" Munion said, surprised.

"Yes."

"They'll know you then," Munion muttered, striking his forehead with the flat of his hand.

They left Long Branch the next morning, parting company with Dr. Pargiter but with the promise of rejoining him far north, in the place he suggested: Franklinville, Massachusetts.

"The mills," Dr. Pargiter said, "opportunities there. Less competition than in Lowell."

Of course, the name was not new to Florilla. Franklinville was the place that Benjamin Bender had left, the place Andrew McKenzie had described to her.

16

They were weeks traveling. Sometimes they stayed at inns, sometimes they slept in the wagon somewhere off the road. Although the nights were getting cold, Florilla preferred sleeping in the wagon. She didn't like the stares and questions of the inn guests, disliked still more Munion's impromptu magic shows. Invariably, he would spend the night drinking with other travelers at the innkeeper's hearth and the next day would find him in a foul temper with a headache that made him swear with every jolt of the wagon. Those days were slow and silent. Sometimes he would rail against the fates that had endowed him with insufficient gifts. At other times, he grew maudlin, and Florilla would have to sit up on the seat beside him while he bemoaned the cruel social structure that had blighted his marriage.

"I loved your mother," he would say, "as much as man ever loved a woman. I never saw anyone as beautiful as she was."

And here he would quote several lines of doggerel verse and brush away tears with the back of his hand as the horse ambled along and the wagon rattled and swayed.

"She came from a fine family," he would continue, snuffling slightly. "That's where you get your haughtiness and the way you carry yourself, my girl.

"That," he would add bitterly, "makes you think you're better than the likes of Jack Munion. But I'll tell you what will earn *your* bread's not any of that fancy breeding, it's the talent you got from me."

He would stare at her with mixture of fury and melancholy and mutter:

"You'd run away if you could. You'd go. You'd leave me to go back to those fancy people, to that old goat Bender with his Latin and Greek, his marble statues and his gardens. All built on the backs of the downtrodden."

"That's not true," Florilla said. "They're happy in the mill. They can earn money. Otherwise they'd be living dirt poor on farms. That's worse."

Munion snorted

"You think so. He brainwashed you. At least on a farm no one's bossing you, walking up and down, watching over you. Nobody owns you."

"But then nature owns you," Florilla said.

Munion glared at her.

"You're a pert one," he said angrily, "I've a mind to give you the back of my hand."

He threatened this so often that she wondered what it was that checked him. Still, she wanted to go north. From Andrew McKenzie's stories, she imagined New England as a cluster of Bendervilles. She liked the idea of helping the mill girls there—it would be something like the healing she had done at Benderville. And somewhere in New England, in that new world, she would finally run away.

In Connecticut, the leaves were beginning to turn. The nights were now too cold for sleeping in the wagon, so they stayed at country inns. At dusk, they would dip into little towns whose white church spires gleamed through the thickening dark. They would follow a servant girl up narrow stairs into bare, cold rooms where there were only the most necessary furnishings and seldom more than a scrap of carpet for comfort. The bed linen was rough, sometimes clean, sometimes not. Mattresses were lumpy and hard, made of straw or horsehair that poked through sharp as needles. But once, near the Massachusetts border, they came into a small town arranged around a common with maples whose scarlet leaves seemed to hold the last sunset light. The inn was Greek Revival in style with four columns and long windows that threw back the light. Florilla caught her breath. It was like a smaller Woodland Place. This inn had fireplaces with crackling fires, even one in her bedroom. Sinking gratefully between the clean-smelling sheets, Florilla, drifting near sleep, saw her room in the mansion at Benderville, heard Ananda and Lethe moving in the kitchen below. Clearly, she saw the study, the statue of Daphne, and then, so clearly that it seemed more than a dream, Benjamin Bender in front of the library window looking out into the dark, at the maple leaves burning bright in the moonlight.

Colin was thunderstruck to find Florilla gone.

"Well, where *is* she?" he said, pacing up and down the length of the drawing room. "She can't have vanished."

"Well, no," said Lady Amberwell, "she went part of the way by canoe."

"Did no one try to find her?"

"No one could. There wasn't a trace, even of the canoe. The children were devastated."

"You can't have looked properly. Was a search party sent out?"

"Yes, of course it was. You forget, Colin, how she came to us. She was running away then. You don't know what that was about. Maybe whatever it was caught up with her."

"*Caught up with her!* You make her sound like some sort of criminal."

"My dear Colin, in this vagabond place one never knows."

"I would have married her," Colin said evenly. "She understood about the orchids. I begin to wonder what hand you had in this."

"Come now," Boffin said, interposing his bulky figure between the two of them, "let's go for a walk, Colin."

They went outside. The afternoon sun of late October sent a golden dazzle through the brown leaves of the oaks, a coruscation, it seemed to Colin, of his own anger, and then of helplessness, the world seen through tears.

"My dear chap," Boffin said, "something very much like this happened to my friend Rosetti with one of those wenches he was always picking off the streets."

"Boffin," Colin said, "I don't want to hear about any of your bloody artist friends."

"Well, that's silly, old fellow, because it's most applicable to this situation."

"Boffin, we are not talking about some prostitute culled from the streets by a decadent, drug-addicted poetaster."

Boffin expostulated but was ignored.

"This was a girl of beauty, of background, who knew more Latin and Greek than you ever will. Not only that, she was most awfully helpful with my work. Once I was gone from here, I realized how much I missed her.

"What I want to know from you, Boffin," Colin went on, seizing the other by the neck of his smock, "is what she was told by all you meddlers? What did Aunt Lou tell her about Amaryllis Court and all that?"

"Well," Boffin said nervously, "just about the greenhouses."

"And?"

"Well, and Sophronia."

"Oh, my God," Colin cried, shoving Boffin away so hard that he fell heavily against a tree.

"Well, good heavens, man," Boffin said irritably, recovering his balance, "you *are* to marry her."

"I would," Colin said calmly, "rather be dead."

"Wait," Boffin said slowly, "Frau Muehlberg!"

Colin raised his hands to the sky.

"Not that old windbag. Not coming again. I can't bear it."

"No, no, man. The letter. The letter she left."

"Letter?"

"For the girl. For Flora."

The letter lay unopened in Lady Amberwell's escritoire. She produced it reluctantly, having, in fact, forgotten all about it.

"Do you think you should open it?" Lady Amberwell said. "Frau Muehlberg said something about the old man being interested in how she acquired her education."

Colin took the letter to his room, which was piled with specimen cases. On an easel stood a careful botanical drawing of *calypso*. Jars bristled with dried grasses, plants recently taken from the press were laid on sheets of blotting paper. It was a strange microcosm of the brittle, desiccated autumn landscape outside. Carefully clearing aside some notes, he sat down at his desk and opened the envelope.

Dear Florilla,

> *We have had today a visitor at Benderville, a Frau Muehlberg, who has described to me the place at which she is staying over by Alice Furnace. I have, of course, long known of the existence of Woodland Place and that it houses many visitors. In her description of one, I thought I recognized you.*

> *If you are happy there, as tutor to the children, then I am glad. My attempt to protect you was, perhaps, misguided. If this letter reaches you, please reply. I do not intend to try to call you back.*

> *Ever your friend and teacher,*
> *Benjamin Bender*

Florilla. Colin turned the name over in his mind. So Flora wasn't even her real name.

17

The Massachusetts farms were neat and tended, surrounded by rich fields stooked with grain. The road by which Florilla and Munion entered the town ran level along the railroad tracks, like the flat edge of the world. An engine had halted, puffing steam and smoke that mingled with the dust kicked up in the street by passing wagons. As Florilla looked up, the town rose out of the vapor, and behind it, ridges of trees blazed red and yellow.

Franklinville was set narrowly in the steep cleft of the Blackstar River. The buildings were mainly red brick, warm in the afternoon sun. The snorting of the train mixed with the clangor of the mills on air that eddied warm and cold like water.

Florilla thought it exciting after the sparse little villages.

"Franklinville," Munion said with satisfaction. "Franklinville, Massachusetts. This is where Pargiter's meeting us. It's a prosperous town. Big gingham mills. We start here, and when we get known, we go on the circuit: Lowell, then Boston, then. . . ." He fixed his eyes on the distance between the horse's ears. "New York. Maybe London, Paris—"

"You can't get there by wagon," Florilla said.

The street wound to the right, and they found themselves laboring up a steep hill with a sheer drop down to the Blackstar River cutting its way through the gorge below.

"Sweet Savior," Munion muttered.

The horse's haunches were trembling, and they had to jump down and walk beside her.

The noise was what struck Florillla, growing as they neared the heart of the town. She could see the huge brick buildings of the mill yard and the tall, Italianate bell tower. The thunder of the machinery was doubled and redoubled, echoed, magnified by the rock walls of the gorge. She realized now that sand and trees must have muffled the sound of the Benderville Mill. That was a gentle receptive, mutable landscape where this was harsh and adamant. This was the town Benjamin Bender had left to create his utopia in the Pines. What a strange chance it was that she should find herself here. This must be what he remembered on those October mornings when he stood under the maples. How different it was from the town in the Pines.

They turned sharply left onto Main Street and stopped to breathe the horse. Main Street ran straight for a distance lined by more shops than Florilla had ever seen in one place. There were drapers and dressmakers, dry goods and furniture stores, a jeweler, a harness shop with shiny trunks set outside on the wooden porch, "Daguerrean artists" whose windows were filled with the sepia likenesses of girls. Somehow, the rows and rows of pictures had an eerie graveyard quality that made her shiver. They passed the Blackstar Hotel and turned up a side street that ran along one side of a small park, planted with trees and crisscrossed by stone paths. Traversing the park was a familiar figure, carrying a plaster head under his arm.

"Now," Munion said, "that's magic." And he pulled the horse to a halt.

Dr. Pargiter hurried on, head down, into the street. Munion took the whip from its socket, and, with a quick flick of the lash, dislodged the phrenologist's hat.

"Pargiter!" he called.

Dr. Pargiter stopped.

"Munion, old fellow!" he cried with genuine enthusiasm. "And the beautiful Rosemalia! How I have been hoping for your arrival! The

pickings have been slim in the phrenology line. Ground too much trod-
den, I fear, so that every wretched country girl thinks she can 'read' her
own head."

"Magic," Munion said, "is what's needed."

"Let me up," said Dr. Pargiter, "and I will show you to our humble
lodgings."

Colin went to Benderville. He rode overland on his uncle's favorite mare,
galloping her more of the way than would have pleased Lord Amberwell.
It was a long ride over causeways, through woods, past lonely farms and
small hamlets. He arrived at Benderville just as the bell rang for the
noon break, causing the mare to shy and balk at the bridge.

From the terrace of the mansion house, Benjamin Bender observed
this incident. The rider expertly urging the horse forward was no local,
and the horse no farm bred. A visitor of consequence approached.
Benjamin Bender waited.

Colin rode up to the mansion gate and dismounted.

"Mr. Bender?" he said.

"The same," said Benjamin Bender.

"My name is Colin Drysdale. I come from the other side of the Pines,
from Woodland Place. Perhaps you know my uncle, Lord Amberwell?"

Benjamin Bender nodded.

"Certainly I know of him," he replied. "We have never met."

"Please, sir," Colin said, "I must talk to you. It is most urgent."

"Come inside," said Benjamin Bender. A sharp wind was blowing
from the river and it was cold on the terrace. "You may leave your horse
here; I'll send for someone to stable it."

The young man settled himself on the other side of the desk where
Florilla had so often sat. Benjamin Bender studied him: a serious, poetic

face, a little too handsome perhaps, the lock of chestnut hair falling across the high, pale forehead. Self-absorbed, Benjamin Bender thought, like most young men, but not really arrogant and seeming, so far as he was capable, to care about Florilla. For it was Florilla he was describing. Benjamin Bender knew that. He had known it when that German woman came to see him and described the visitor to Woodland Place.

The young man had stopped talking, and Benjamin Bender had to wrench his mind back from the memories of the child, the girl, the young woman bent over her books.

"I asked if you thought this girl was your ward, sir?"

"Yes," Benjamin Bender said. He felt too tired, suddenly, to say any more. He left the bare word in the air.

"I see," Colin said uncertainly.

The old man looked drained, almost ill. Colin glanced around the room at the shelves of books. His eyes rested on the marble Daphne now catching the midday light. He thought of Boffin's painting and the pang it gave him at every meal: Florilla's face, Florilla fleeing, as perhaps she was now.

"Then where," Colin said desperately, "where could she have gone? Where could she be?"

Benjamin Bender shrugged his shoulders wearily.

"My boy," he said, "I have no way of knowing that, any more than I knew where she had gone when she left here. She must have more than a touch of the wandering heredity."

"Wandering heredity?"

"Her father is a gypsy character. A magician. A traveler. I hope he has no hand in this."

"Is it likely? She never mentioned him."

"It's not likely that she would. She hates him, but she is of considerable value to him for her healing powers. She could vastly improve his act."

Colin leaned forward, turning the full intensity of his gaze on the old man.

"You mean that he could have kidnapped her?"

Following directions from Benjamin Bender, Colin rode to Sim Place. He dismounted in the clearing and stared at the blind face of the shack. This was where the child Florilla had lived alone with her dying grandmother. Though mingled pity and respect filled his heart, he also noticed the trees and the usual indigenous bushes. The floor of the clearing was mossy, the sort of place to look for the curly grass fern, and it was October, the time to look for it. Stooping, he crisscrossed the open ground. He found not the curly grass fern but the fronds of *habenaria*. He knelt down to be sure. There was no doubt. Here the *habenaria* grew. This was why his extra press was missing. She must have come here the afternoon she left Woodland Place, to find it for him. Was the man, Munion, there? Could he have caught her?

Colin ran back to the shack, pulling at the door with all his strength till the hinges gave. The scene inside confirmed all. Someone had lived there recently. There were bedclothes on the beds and dishes on the table. She had come to get the *habenaria* for him, and Munion had caught her and taken her with him. Anguish seized him, and he leaned helplessly against the door frame. He had caused this by his carelessness. He turned from the sight of her imprisonment, pulling the warped door closed behind him. But why had she not escaped. How could Munion have kept her prisoner against her will to use her in his tawdry act?

She must not have wanted to get away, must not have wanted to come back to him. This last thought was as crushing as a physical blow. *She had not wanted to come back to him.*

Benjamin Bender put Colin up for the night since it was growing dark by the time he returned from Sim Place.

"The *habenaria*," Colin blurted over the soup course. "She must have gone there to find it for me. She said she knew where it grew and I found the leaves."

"Ah yes, Benjamin Bender said, "the *Habenaria integra*. I have been told by the schoolmaster, who dabbles in botany, that it grows at Sim Place."

"He must have been there," Colin said, "and caught her. The magician."

Benjamin Bender nodded.

"Very probable,"

"Someone had clearly been living in the shack. But how could he have held her against her will? She must have agreed to go with him."

"Perhaps."

"Sir," Colin said feverishly. "She loved me. I know she loved me."

"I can't," Benjamin Bender said, "speak to that. But is there anything anyone could have said to her that might have made her feel—well—that perhaps you had deceived her and that you didn't love her?"

"Oh, my God." Colin said.

"You're a very foolish boy," Lady Amberwell said crossly. "I had to tell her if you weren't going to do it."

They were alone in Lady Amberwell's bedroom. It was the hour before dinner, and she was sitting at her escritoire while Colin paced back and forth. The curtains were still open so that everything was flushed with sunset light.

"How did you *know* I wasn't going to do it? How did you *know* I wasn't going to break the engagement?"

Lady Amberwell shrugged impatiently.

"My dear Colin, that would be impossible. Putting aside the commotion and unhappiness, even scandal, it would cause, there is no other way that you can keep Amaryllis Court."

At once he turned on her.

"Did it ever occur to you," he said, "that without Florilla I might not *want* to keep Amaryllis Court?"

Lady Amberwell sighed.

"These passions don't last, you know. I should have thought you old enough to understand that. In a month, you'll have forgotten her."

"I'll never forget," Colin said furiously. "I would as soon forget the *Habenaria integra.*"

"Well, I don't know about that, but you will realize as you get older that the individual is not as important as you think. Families are important. And houses like this one and like Amaryllis Court."

Colin left the room.

18

I n the evenings in Franklinville, Florilla, Munion, and Dr. Pargiter made the rounds of the boarding houses, providing phrenology and magic tricks. Franklinville was a source of some fascination to Florilla, so different was it from Benderville. As they passed up and down the streets, they met the practitioners and propounders of many other arts: galvanism, the water cure, character reading, Dr. Graham's Diet, motley figures flitting along, carrying bags, pushing barrows. The world came to the bigger town as it never had to the village in the Pines.

After dinner in the mill's boarding houses, the tables were pulled back, and some of the girls sat around sewing and knitting or reading by the weak lamplight. Others went up to bed, and some had the energy to go out "on the street," where the shops stayed open till nine o'clock. It was then that the mountebanks came into the parlors to pitch their cures, ply their trades.

In Benderville, there had been only one boarding house for women and one for men, and the major entertainment had been sallies back and forth between the neat front gardens of each. Benjamin Bender had allowed none of this sort of hurly-burly. The girls of Benderville had been little different from the girls of its surrounding farms; they simply went to the mill of a morning rather than to the fields. Here in Franklinville, there was a great deal more sophistication. The new girls, the "green" ones, were desperate to "get the rust off," to doff their homespun dresses and shawls for the Merrimack print and bugle-beaded cloaks offered by the stores on Main Street.

They took to vigorous self-improvement in many forms, from the study of languages and other academic subjects, the attending of lyceum lectures, the writing of essays and poetry, to teaching in the sabbath schools. Some few became committed "do-gooders," vying with the likes of Munion for their cohorts' money in the name of Indian missions or, nearer to home, the Hibernian Relief Society. For the soft-hearted, it was a toss-up whether stockings and ribbons or the needy would lay first claim to what money they didn't send home.

Munion was a great success with the mill girls. They preferred his magic to phrenology and him to Dr. Pargiter. Best of all, they loved Florilla. Blind-folded, she read the cards they chose, told them the names of their brothers and sisters at home. They gasped and gave little screams of delight. They also loved to hold the black hen and the rabbit, reminders of life on the farm.

"We'll build things up," Munion said, "before we start the healing."

On this particular night he was in an expansive mood as they turned off Chestnut Street to walk down Grove Street between the identical rows of two-story brick boarding houses.

"With the reputation we've been getting for our parlor tricks," he said, "I should think we could get the Lyceum soon for a big show."

Dr. Pargiter nodded vigorously.

"We should emphasize the healing again. With the beautiful Rosemalia."

He leered at Florilla.

As they climbed the steps of one of the houses, a girl stuck her head out of the door and ran back inside, slamming it behind her.

"The magician's coming!" they heard her cry. "The magician's coming!"

Through the window, they saw the obedient heads bent to books or handwork, rise in expectation. Several of the younger girls jumped to their feet. Munion, whistling, knocked cheerfully on the door.

As soon as they came into the parlor, Florilla noticed the girl. She sat apart from the others, head resting on her hand. She was clearly in pain.

Munion began his spiel, arousing giggles of excitement, Dr. Pargiter hauled his plaster head out of its bag, while Florilla went over to the girl.

"What's wrong?" she said.

The girl squinted up at her.

"It's my head," she answered in a hoarse whisper. "Some days it gets so bad that I almost pass out at my looms. They had to half carry me home today. And it won't stop aching. It's no good me lying down. It don't help."

"Just sit still," Florilla said, "I'm going to help you. Now just let me lift your head."

"Oh, miss," the girl wailed, "don't move it. If you move it, I'll pass out."

"Please trust me," Florilla said. Going behind her and placing one hand on either side of the girl's skull, she lifted her head out of her hands. The girl gave one little cry and fell silent.

"Close your eyes," Florilla said gently.

Holding the girl's head, feeling the skull beneath the soft hair made Florilla's hands tingle, then gradually grow numb. This was how she sensed the sources of pain. Slowly, if the healing were working, the feeling would come back into her own fingers. She closed her eyes. For a moment, she was aware of nothing, not the room she stood in, not the people around her. She saw flickering glimpses of Benderville and Woodland Place. When the feeling came back into her hands and she opened her eyes, the whole room was hushed. Munion and Dr. Pargiter merely stood there, Munion holding a handful of silk scarves, Pargiter with his hand on the plaster head. All the eyes of all the girls were on her.

"My head," the girl said, "it's stopped hurting!"

She turned large, startled eyes on Florilla.

"It's gone! I feel so free and light! Oh, tell me it won't come back!"

"I can't be sure of that," Florilla said, "but I can come back a few times in the next week or two and see if that will help."

Immediately, there was a crowding round her of other girls, complaining of sore backs, leg cramps, stiff shoulders. Florilla turned from one to another until Munion stopped it.

"Ladies, girls," he said. "Rosemalia is able to heal, but she was only giving you an example tonight. Regular healing sessions will be set up and payment will be necessary."

Dr. Pargiter nodded vigorously, holding the plaster head as though he were healing that.

"Well, when can we see her?" several called.

"Steady now," Munion said, "times will have to be arranged."

It was the healing that eventually got them the Lyceum stage, normally reserved for visiting lecturers. For several weeks, Florilla had healed by appointment in the basement of the Congregational Church. Then Munion persuaded the Lyceum Committee to hold healing evenings. In the brief hours between the ringing out and the curfew bell that summoned them back to their boarding houses, girls streamed in. It was exhausting work, but Florilla was glad for the exhaustion that left her floating beyond thought, able to go to her room and fall asleep at once.

One morning while Munion and Dr. Pargiter still slept, Florilla left the boarding house and walked down toward the river and the mills. She paused on the bridge over the Blackstar to look up at the brick building of the Blackstar Mill. As she watched, an old man came out of the main door and stood looking at his watch. At that moment, she heard the whistle of an approaching train. The old man nodded in satisfaction and went inside. She knew that it was Isaiah Bender and for a moment she wanted to run after him. But she stayed where she was.

On one evening a few weeks later, Munion announced that they would be leaving in a matter of days for Lowell.

"They want us on the stage at the Lyceum there. Just us. Nothing else on the bill."

"Think of it," breathed Dr. Pargiter, "and all due to our Rosemalia."

He looked at Florilla with moist eyes as he and Munion poured glasses from a bottle of whiskey.

"Who knows who'll see us!" Munion said. "Lowell's a much bigger place. Maybe the son of some mill owner'll fall for you, Florilla, and then you can look after me in my old age."

He reached out to pinch her arm, but she flinched away, while Dr. Pargiter laughed till he nearly choked and had to be thumped on the back.

"Don't worry," Munion shouted, "if you die, Rosemalia'll bring you back. We could put that in the act."

The two of them snorted with laughter.

"When are we leaving?" Florilla asked.

"Day after tomorrow. You got one more healing session tomorrow night."

Colin tried to find her. Benjamin Bender suggested Long Branch.

"The season will have ended," he said, "but that's the most likely place for them to have gone. I'm told that Munion's done shows there before."

Long Branch was deserted. Riding down Ocean Avenue, Colin passed only one farm wagon and a few people on foot, making it hard to imagine the density of carriage and foot traffic the season would have seen.

Since the boardwalk seemed a logical beginning, he tied his horse to the promenade railing and walked down it. The sea was gray and calm, curling over the rocks of the jetty. The pier was empty, all the shops were closed. On a hoarding, a few salt stained flyers fluttered. One of them caught his eye.

MUNION THE MAGICIAN
AND THE BEAUTIFUL ROSEMALIA
PSYCHIC READER AND MEDIUM

DR. I. A. PARGITER
WORLD RENOWNED PHRENOLOGIST

"Rosemalia," Colin whispered, "Florilla, Flora."

There the trail went cold. Colin inquired at the hotel named on the flyer. Yes, they had been there, but no one knew where they had gone.

"Maybe they headed for the city. That show of theirs was making money. The magician said something about Philadelphia."

Colin rode back to Woodland Place, arriving exhausted and travel-stained, only to leave the next morning for Philadelphia. He walked the streets of that city for two days, but no one had seen or head of Munion the magician and the beautiful Rosemalia. He advertised for information in the papers in Philadelphia and New York. No one answered.

November came. Impatient letters began to arrive from Erasmus Scrubdale, Colin's future father-in-law, requesting the date of his return. Writing to Lady Amberwell, he suggested that Colin was not taking his responsibilities seriously. Colin also had a letter from his father, Lord Fenhope, largely cataloguing the waterfowl he had seen in the park of Amaryllis Court in the last two months, but containing, in the last two sentences, some vague reference to Colin's obligations. Sophronia, herself, did not write.

Colin, however, received another letter far more to his liking from two distinguished English botanists, Dr. Cutler and Dr. Boothroyd, both of whom had taught him at Oxford. They were planning an orchid expedition to South America sponsored by the Regina and Paradise Nurseries, Holloway, London. They wanted him to join them in December. The expedition would be of at least a year's duration. Colin accepted at once. He saw no point in living in North America without Florilla or in England with Sophronia Scrubdale. It was a once-in-a-lifetime opportunity, a perfect botanical excuse, and so he wrote to Sophronia regretfully postponing his return. Lady Amberwell threw up her hands; Colin was adamant. Boffin began a painting called *Goddess of the Amazon.*

19

Lowell was Franklinville on a huge scale, set on flat land unlike the gorges of the Blackstar. On the bridge over the wide, rushing Merrimack River, Munion pulled the horse up and pointed his whip.

"You've never been in a city this big," he said.

"As a matter of fact," Dr. Pargiter said, "I've been to Philadelphia.
"Well, so have I," said Jack Munion, "but there wasn't the opportunity there, Pargiter, the opportunity."

Florilla sat in the back of the wagon, stroking the black hen's wing through the slats of her cage. It was November now, and soon all travel would become difficult. She supposed that they would be in Lowell for the winter—Lowell or Boston. The winter would be hard and cold, snow and ice. She thought about November in the Pines, the pines still green, the blackjack oaks holding their brown leaves. She missed it. She didn't want to be cut off from it for a whole winter. She thought of the haze of woodsmoke on those first cold nights at Benderville. She thought of the firewood wagon, delivering logs to each of the cottages. She remembered the fire in the library as she worked on her Latin and Greek.

Munion chose the Appleton Hotel, one of the city's best.

"Appearances are important," he said. "In a place this size you have to make people notice you."

They had three small rooms at the back of the top floor. Still, like everyone else, they walked in through the big front doors with the frosted glass, across the marble floor of the hall, past the potted palms and up the wide mahogany stairs. Though the stairs became meaner on the leg to the top floor, the rooms were clean, with pictures on the walls and comfortable feather beds.

Florilla awoke early to the ringing of the mill bells. It seemed to her, struggling up from sleep, that she must be in some huge belfry. She got out of bed and went to the window that overlooked the street. Since the hotel was one of the taller buildings, she had a good view out over the town. Girls poured down the streets toward the mills, in whose towers the bells rang. If there had seemed to be hordes of girls in Franklinville, Lowell was beyond imagining. Among them, she noticed many groups of girls or women, shabbily dressed, dragging children by the hand. Clearly, here was no benevolent despotism like Benjamin Bender's.

"Sit down, boy," Munion said, beckoning to the waiter. "Have breakfast with us, and I will tell you about the most amazing act in the whole United States."

"That's all right, sir," said the young reporter from *The Lowell Courier* in a flustered way, his eye on Florilla. "I've already had my breakfast."

"Well, another cup of coffee never hurt," said Munion, perceiving the object of his attention. "This young lady here is the beautiful Rosemalia, psychic and healer."

The young man began scribbling in a notebook he carried.

"We're appearing at the Lyceum. In two nights time. Just us. We've got the whole program."

Dr. Pargiter cleared his throat.

"Oh yes," Munion said, "including, of course, our friend the phrenologist here. He's part of the act. As am I."

He reached out and drew a dollar bill from behind the young man's ear.

"Now listen, boy. "Do you know of anywhere I can get some hand-bills printed?"

"Why yes," the boy stammered. "Why yes, sir, I believe we could do it down at the press."

The next evening, Florilla found herself on a windy corner, shivering in her beaded velvet cloak, at the mills' ringing out time. Beside her, Munion handed out handbills to girls who stared at her curiously as they hurried by. Florilla felt ridiculous and, even more, humiliated. She longed to get away. The numbness that had followed her discoveries about Colin was wearing off. There might no longer be anything for her at Woodland Place, but certainly there was nothing for her with Munion. Only the healing enabled her to bear it at all. But if she did run away, where could she go? Surely not all the way back to Benderville.

By the time of their Lyceum appearance, word had already spread over the complex grapevine that linked the mill towns of Massachusetts. News of the healer had spread from sisters to cousins to friends who had left the smaller towns for Lowell. On top of that, there had been the article in *The Lowell Courier*, and the handbills.

Munion opened the act with his magic, but he had scarcely cracked an egg and produced the black hen when the crowd began to call for Florilla.

"Rosemalia!" they chanted. "Rosemalia. We want the healer!"

Quickly snatching a bouquet of paper flowers from the air, Munion bowed and spread his arms, signaling the crowd to be quiet.

"Very well. I bow to your desires. I will bring you the extraordinary, the gifted Rosemalia."

Backstage, Dr. Pargiter shook Florilla by the shoulder. Annoyed that he had had no chance to go on with his phrenology, he pushed her roughly forward. Florilla walked into the lights and stood at the edge of the stage facing the murmuring crowd.

"Now," said Munion, "before the healing, we will have a demonstration of Rosemalia's psychic powers."

He called up a small, rabbity looking girl from the front row, and Florilla told her where she came from, the names of her brothers and sisters. The crowd murmured again. Then they began to surge toward the stage. Watching them come, Florilla was frightened. She saw in their faces so much anguish, sallow skin stretched taut over the bones, lit from behind by the exploding lights and colors of pain.

"One at a time," Munion was shouting. "Get in line, ladies, please!"

But they pushed past him, climbing the steps to the stage, crowding round Florilla, reaching out to pull at her dress.

"I can only help you one at a time," Florilla said with greater calm than she felt. "You must come individually, please!"

They jostled obediently into line.

"It's my lungs, Miss Rosemalia," said the first one. "I can hardly get my breath sometimes. Soon they say I won't be able to work in the weave room in summer when the windows are shut and the air's so heavy to breathe."

Florilla worked for three hours, healing one after another. By the end of it, she was light-headed, and her legs felt too weak to hold her up. But the crowd was quiet, awed, and Munion was able to send them away with a promise that the healing would be continued on a regular schedule.

They were booked at the Lyceum for several weeks running. Munion rented space in the basement of another church and set up more healing sessions. Money was again rolling in. Florilla felt a pang each time she saw a girl drop her few coins into Dr. Pargiter's eager hands. Invitations came from mill owners and overseers for private shows in the mansions of Belmont Avenue. These houses reminded Florilla of Woodland Place, and it always seemed that Colin might appear amid one of these genteel groups, men in frock coats, women with their jewels and their tartan silks.

They moved into a handsome suite of rooms on the second floor of the hotel. Munion allowed her more time to herself now; he seemed less worried that she would try to escape. Florilla supposed that that was because she would find it harder. Already she was well-known in Lowell, even in the Paddy camps, as the shantytowns where the Irish immigrants lived were called.

Florilla was sorry for Lowell's mill girls. They were terrified of illness. Illness that cut their efficiency meant dismissal, being sent home to those stony farms in New Hampshire and Vermont. Serious illness could mean going into the hospital. The hospital cost three dollars a week, a week's wages, which was paid by the corporation but had to be repaid by the operative. To the mill girls, this was a staggering and terrifying debt. They could not afford to be ill. Florilla thought of the special sick rooms set apart in the boarding houses at Benderville, the kindly ministrations of Dr. Peace, the wagons always ready for the trip to the hospital at Tuckerton in serious cases. All without charge. It was to protest this kind of exploitation that Benjamin Bender had first gone south to build his utopia in the Pines. She thought often of how appalled he would be by the pain and terror in those young faces, by the pale children, the bobbin doffers, who went every day, all day to the mills with scant hope of schooling. Even the mill buildings themselves were huge brick industrial palaces, out of human scale.

Since the wizard and the phrenologist were late risers, Florilla often went early for a walk, or on sunny days, to sit in a nearby park. On recent mornings, she had noticed a shadowy figure, a woman wrapped in a heavy shawl, lingering near the park railings. When she finally approached, the shawl covering all but her eyes, Florilla smiled at her.

"Please, miss," she said in a lilting accent, "are you the healer then?"

Florilla looked into the dark, sunken eyes and nodded.

"My baby, miss. He's poorly and feverish. I can't soothe him. I've no money to give you. I can only beg."

Getting up quickly, Florilla touched the woman's shoulder.

"I will come."

They made their way through almost empty streets, to the north beyond the mills where the Paddy camps were built on swampland near the Western Canal. The air was thick with coal smoke, and Florilla had to hold her own shawl over her mouth. The woman led her into one of the wooden shanties, through a cramped hallway where she glimpsed a number of dirty, half-naked children. They entered a room where an old woman sat alone mumbling a rosary next to a battered cradle. The woman reached into it and handed Florilla a filthy, skeletal baby.

"It's hard to keep him clean, miss," she said. "It's a long way to the pump."

Florilla put her hands on the baby's chest until it breathed more easily. She left promising to come the next day.

For several days, before Munion found out, she went every morning. The baby improved, but as word spread, others came—children and old women mostly. The men were out laboring as builders, and many of the younger women had begun working in the mills.

Munion was furious.

"Wasting your time and energy on trash," he snarled. "They've no money to pay. They work for less in the mills, soon they'll drive the Yankee girls out. You'll get sick yourself going down there in all their filth."

"If I could choose," Florilla said, "I would never charge for healing. It's wrong that we do."

"Don't take that high tone with me, girl. What do you think gives you a warm bed and food on the table?"

Florilla didn't answer.

"Well, I think we'll be keeping a closer eye on you from now on, won't we Pargiter?"

"Why, yes," Dr. Pargiter mumbled, "we wouldn't want anything to happen to you."

Florilla saw the woman once again as she was leaving the Lyceum in the evening.

"The baby's well, miss," she whispered. "This is all I can give you."

Into Florilla's hand she pressed a tiny carving of a pig.

"Bog oak," she said. "T'will bring you luck."

"Hey!" Munion shouted coming down the steps.

Like a shadow, the woman was gone.

20

"They want us in Boston," Munion crowed.

It was the week before Christmas, and he and Dr. Pargiter were sitting in front of a comfortable fire in their hotel room. Florilla sat at a table by the window watching the sunset deepen the red of the brick buildings across the street.

"Think of it," Dr. Pargiter said, "being on a real stage with proper footlights."

"It's where we belong, Pargiter. I can see the billing: MUNION, THE WIZARD OF THE PINES. PREPARE TO BE AMAZED AND CONFOUNDED."

"And PARGITER, THE WIZARD OF PHRENOLOGY," said Dr. Pargiter, and they both laughed.

"Will I be healing in Boston?" Florilla asked.

"I think we'll cut some of that," Munion said. "More of the guessing games and the tricks."

"I don't know, Munion," Dr. Pargiter said. "It's the healing they want."

"Whatever's to be done," Munion said jovially to Florilla, "you'll do it."

The journey from Lowell to Boston had been hard going, roads patched with ice and frozen into solid ruts. Dr. Pargiter had been in favor of taking the train, but Munion had said it was too difficult to transport the props and animals without the wagon.

By dusk on the first day, they reached Concord where they were to spend the night at the inn. Alighting from the wagon, exhausted by the cold and the constant jolting and jarring, Florilla found the little town beautiful: frame houses neatly fenced, windows warm with light, the scurrying shadows of people going from house to house on holiday errands. The inn was cheerful with jars of holly and swags of pine and laurel. Fires blazed in all the fireplaces. The wizard and the phrenologist settled happily in front of the one in the tavern room.

The phrenologist sized up people's heads, thereby drawing them into the conversation, while Munion made small objects disappear, only to pull them out of people's ears. They immediately became the center of much interest and jollity among the guests, but Florilla was so sleepy that she asked the serving girl to show her to her room.

It was a small room, cozy with lamplight and the glow from the fire. Florilla immediately got ready for bed. She had just climbed into the four poster and blown out the lamp when she heard the singing. Florilla got up and went to the window. Below, under the dark elms, the carolers stood, glowing like will-o-the-wisps in the wavering light of the candles they carried. Their voices rose eerily in the brittle air with a sound not entirely human. She stayed at the window till they had finished singing, and not till they had dispersed, candles bobbling away into the dark, did she go back to bed.

On a wall opposite the livery stable in Boston they saw the first poster:

JACK MUNION
THE WIZARD OF THE PINES
*MAGIC * SLEIGHT OF HAND*

DR. I.A. PARGITER
WORLD-RENOWNED PHRENOLOGIST
PRESENT
THE BEAUTIFUL ROSEMALIA

WHOSE PSYCHIC POWERS WILL ASTOUND YOU
*SPIRITUALIST * MEDIUM * HEALER*

It was only one of many that they saw about the city, on railings, on walls, in windows. Sometimes there were knots of people gathered reading, and sometimes, Munion, dragging Florilla by the arm, would swagger up to them and tell them who he was.

Munion was gambling. He had begun gambling in Lowell when there was first an excess of money. He was an astute card player and had made this known when his magic took him into the mansions of the rich. His successes had provided him with introductions in Boston. The first night they were there, he and Dr. Pargiter locked Florilla in her room at their lodgings and went out. Florilla did not know where they were going, but she was happy enough to be left on her own. Sometimes she allowed herself to think about Colin; always she saw him in some high mountain place where fantastic orchids hung from trees.

At dawn, she was woken by the return of her father and the phrenologist. They were clearly drunk and arguing, or, rather, the phrenologist was attempting to reason with the wizard.

"I can win," she heard Munion say. He repeated it several times.

In the darkness, made shallow by the reflection of the streetlights, Florilla lay very still.

There was more pounding and thumping, heavy crashes that meant Munion had thrown his boots against the wall, and the thin, anxious voice of Dr. Pargiter, begging him to get into bed. There was another crash of overturned furniture, then footsteps, the wavering light of an oil lamp under the door. Then all was stilled to vague mutterings, though the phrenologist's voice droned on for a time, weaving in and out of Florilla's restless sleep.

"Get up!" Florilla shouted, banging on the door between the rooms. "Unlock this door. I want some breakfast."

She jumped back as some heavy projectile crashed against the connecting door.

"It's all right, my dear," she heard Dr. Pargiter's voice. "I'm coming to unlock the door."

"Watch her," she heard Munion growl. "Keep your eye on her, Pargiter. Don't trust—" The rest was slurred, and soon the key turned in the lock, and the door opened on a disheveled, agitated Dr. Pargiter.

"Let's have some breakfast, my dear," he said in a nervous whisper. "There are things we should discuss."

"I can't have any more of that sort of thing," the landlady said, poised by the breakfast table in the bay window. "I don't have to put up with it. I've never had any trouble getting lodgers." She drew a quick breath. "I was warned about theater people, but the young lady here is so educated and polite, and you as well, sir, that I thought 'never mind if the other one's a bit rough.'"

"It won't happen again, Mrs. Maltby," the professor said.

"We are sorry," Florilla said.

When Mrs. Maltby had gone, leaving them to their breakfast, Dr. Pargiter leaned forward.

"I'm worried, Miss Florilla," he said. "Your father is gambling heavily. He could sustain heavy losses."

"No doubt," Florilla said. "But there's not much way of stopping him."

"I am insisting on a part of the gate for this performance, and if you will stand with me, I will be able to provide for you if something happens to your father."

Dr. Pargiter gazed at her with moist-eyed eagerness.

"I should like to provide for you, Miss Florilla," he said.

"I can provide for myself, thank you, Dr. Pargiter," Florilla said coldly.

The Christmas performance was an overwhelming success. The hall was packed, and Munion was sober and concentrating. If he was slightly on edge, it only served to give his performance greater bravura. The crowd seemed to enjoy the magic as much as the psychic reading, and even the phrenological demonstration was much applauded.

When the act was over, they were at last on the street, the caged animals in a wheelbarrow. By the time they had returned them to the livery stable, it was snowing quite hard, thick, heavy flakes that had already whitened the street and lay in little heaps on the shoulders of statues.

"You go back to the hotel," Munion said to them, "I'll be home in a few hours."

"Now, Jack," Dr. Pargiter began.

But Jack Munion, the Wizard of the Pines, had turned on his heel, and the last they saw of him was an indistinct figure, cape drawn round him against the falling snow.

When he did not reappear within twenty-four hours, Dr. Pargiter made enquiries. The doors of the rich were shut in his face, though he did manage to retrieve his share of the take from the theater.

Two days passed, and it was Christmas. Bells rang out, and trees decorated with tinsel garlands and lighted candles stood in the bay windows of houses on Commonwealth Avenue.

Over the plum pudding, as the few other boarders who were not with their families dozed lightly near the fire, Dr. Pargiter suggested to Florilla that they join forces.

"I can't imagine, Miss Florilla, that you are grieving greatly for your father, the way you've been treated," he said pompously, as though he himself had had no part in it.

"I'm sure," said Florilla, "that he is not gone for good. We have more shows to do."

"That's just it! I suggest we go on with the act. We don't need him and his paper flowers and feather dusters." Dr. Pargiter snapped his fingers. "It's *you* they come to see, my beautiful Rosemalia."

Florilla recoiled in disgust.

"I'm not your beautiful anything. And if my father is gone, I'm free to go myself."

"And where would you go?" asked Dr. Pargiter, not altogether kindly.

"To work," Florilla said. "I don't mind work. I would go to work in the mills. And if my father's gone, then everything of his is mine: the animals, the wagon, the horse, and all the magic paraphernalia. I shall take it and go."

"Not in this snow you won't," said Dr. Pargiter turning nasty. "I always said the bump of stubbornness was overdeveloped in you."

Then he began to plead.

"Stay with me. We'll be famous. After Boston, then New York, then Europe. Don't you want to see Paris, Rome, London?"

The thought of traveling with Dr. Pargiter was worse than with her father.

"I don't need to see the capitals of Europe," Florilla said. "I only need to make my own life."

Munion didn't return, and the date for their next show was fast approaching. Dr. Pargiter kept a nervous eye on Florilla. He was frightened of what Munion would do if he were to return and find her gone. He paid for her board but refused to give her any cash. Florilla knew, however, where he kept his money. The phrenological head was hollow and had a plate on the bottom which slid back. She waited for the inevitable evening when he got drunk and fell into a deep sleep, forgetting to lock the door between their rooms. At dawn, she tiptoed in. She glanced briefly at him, snoring where he had fallen on the bed. His head looked knobbier than the model's. She took the money and left. No one in the house was stirring.

She went straight to the livery stable to collect horse and wagon, rabbit, doves, and the black hen. Munion had, of course, paid nothing in advance so that some of her money went to settling the bill. With the horse harnessed, the animals in their cages stowed away, she was faced with choosing a destination. She told the ostler she was on her way back to Lowell but headed south instead.

She had studied the route on the map, but she knew it would not be safe to stay on the main road for long. When she came to an intersecting road that looked passable with wagon tracks visible in the fallen snow, she turned west. The night was silent with no wind. The only sounds were the horse's hooves and the creaking of the wagon. These were magnified in Florilla's ears so they seemed to reverberate like an army of horses and wagons. Occasionally, she would stop the mare and hold her hand over her nostrils to see if she could catch, in the still air, any other human sound. The road she had chosen ran level through woods so thick that the tangle of leafless branches almost obscured the sky. After a time, her feet cold and wet, Florilla clambered onto the seat of the wagon and drove on. Gradually, the trees thinned and the road forked. She took the left fork which led away from a cluster of farms into more woods. As the sun came up, promising to warm her cramped toes and fingers, Florilla began to look for a place to stop. At last, she found another track leading off the road. Amid scrubby second growth, she could make out the ruins of a stone wall. These were abandoned farm fields, and one of them was still clear enough for her to turn the wagon into it.

After unhitching and tethering the mare, she lay down on the narrow bed in the wagon, pulling the heavy blankets over her. The rustlings of the rabbit and the birds were comforting. She wasn't very worried. She doubted that Dr. Pargiter would have the ambition to go after her, or, if he did, that he would have the imagination to take this odd, circuitous route. She was not even sure herself where she was going except it would be in a southwesterly direction, maybe to one of those river valleys in Connecticut where there were mills. Then she could work and earn her own bread. She thought no further than this before falling asleep.

21

Florilla woke to hear voices, a strange sort of babble out of which she could make no distinct words. Quickly, she went to open the caravan door. White swirls of mist rose from the snow and it seemed that the small creatures standing before her must have materialized from it. Were they gnomes, elves, or mortal children? They stood in a line, arranged like a small team of ponies, two by two between two ropes that were tied round the waists of the two children at the head and foot of the line. They were dressed exactly alike in gray cloaks, and all had hair cut identically below the ears, so Florilla couldn't tell whether they were boys or girls.

The babbling ceased when they saw her at the top of the steps. They stared at her with unguarded surprise. Florilla was so stunned by the appearance of such extraordinary beings that she did not immediately realize that they were accompanied by two ordinary adults, who now stepped forward. Both were girls, not much older than Florilla, dressed in dark blue capes and bonnets.

"Who are you, please?" one of them asked.

"Flora," Florilla said, using the name she had used at Woodland Place, "Flora Homer, but, please, who are you?"

"These are children from the Hinton School," the second girl said, "and you are on school land."

"I'm sorry," Florilla said. "It was dark when I stopped. I didn't realize. Where is the school?"

The girl turned and pointed. Beyond a line of trees at the end of the meadow stood a large building with a tower.

"What kind of school is it?"

"A training school for the feebleminded."

Florilla looked down at the faces turned up to her. She smiled, they smiled back. Several dropped the rope to clap their hands, then looked bewildered.

"Rope," their companions muttered, poking them. "Rope!"

"Perhaps you would like to see the school," said the girl who had spoken first. "Miss Goodspeed likes visitors. We don't get many."

"And there will be more snow," she added. "Perhaps you will want a place to stay."

Florilla hesitated. In her bones, she wanted warmth and safety. She shook herself.

"The animals," she said. "I can't leave them."

"Of course not. We have barns where they will be safe."

Florilla harnessed the mare. The children looked on in fascination.

"Children, come," the girl said, and the little procession fell into line, Florilla following leading the horse and wagon.

They crossed the field on a track that led through the line of trees into a courtyard in front of the building with the tower. Barns and out-buildings surrounded it, beyond them fields and the outline of a large, winterkilled garden.

The big barn was warm and smelled of hay. The occupants were cows and sheep and a pair of curious goats. One girl had taken the children into the tower building, the other came with Florilla. There was room for the wagon and two big empty box stalls, one for the horse, one for the other animals. Florilla felt more relief at getting them to safety than she felt for herself. Once the animals were settled, she followed the girl outside. The drifting fog and the low, snow-threatening sky seemed ominous.

"I'll take you to Miss Goodspeed," the girl said. "She will be in her office."

Florilla looked up at the tower as they climbed the steps to the heavy mahogany doors.

With a shudder, the bell in the tower began ringing.

"What is that for?" Florilla asked.

"First session," the girl answered. "After breakfast and physical exercise."

They entered a large vestibule, at its center, a statue of a boy with his arm around a wolf.

Romulus or Remus?

Doors suddenly opened off the hall, and streams of children of various ages crossed from one to another.

Florilla followed her guide upstairs.

The door to Miss Goodspeed's office stood open. Miss Goodspeed herself sat at her desk.

"Ma'am," the girl said, "we found her and her wagon in the west field."

She dipped a quick curtsy and ran off.

Florilla and Miss Goodspeed faced each other.

Florilla saw a woman in her sixties with a thin pale face and startling gray eyes. She could only wonder what Miss Goodspeed saw in the girl who stood before her, disheveled in a snow-spattered cloak.

"In the west field," Miss Goodspeed said. "Were you walking? Were you lost?"

"No," Florilla said. "I have a horse and wagon. Not really lost, no."

"Well, then," Miss Goodspeed said, "I'll ask no more. I expect you need breakfast. I'll take you down to the refectory."

The refectory was a large room with a number of tables, each set for eight. Florilla could hear the clatter of dishes and murmur of talk from the kitchen. When Miss Goodspeed opened the door, the hush was immediate.

"Bring our guest whatever she would like."

To Florilla she said:

"Come back to my office when you've had breakfast."

When Florilla returned, the fog had lifted, and a cold December sunlight came through the windows, draining the last color from Miss Goodspeed's pale face. Florilla felt the force of her will and dedication, but also a slipping, a mortal tiredness.

"Well, since you have found us," Miss Goodspeed said, pulling herself together, "let me show you what we do. The bust on the bookcase is of our founder, Dr. Goddard."

The marble bust was like the ones at Benderville, without the laurel wreath.

From the windows, Miss Goodspeed pointed out lawns with plantings of laurel and rhododendron, the barns and outbuildings, the dark border of the woods.

"We have a farm that provides everything we eat," she said, indicating the surrounding fields. "Some of the children like to work with the animals. Yours will be quite safe with them."

Florilla followed Miss Goodspeed down the stairs and into the classrooms. Long windows filled the rooms with light. Big tables replaced desks. Low tiers of shelves ran around the walls. Miss Goodspeed showed her the contents of those shelves: wooden toys and geometric shapes, nesting boxes, blocks in graduated sizes. The children could be taught through the physical manipulation of size, shape, and color. On the tables were simple puzzles, a board for matching colors. The furniture in the classrooms of each age group was carefully built to scale.

"These children learn through the body. That is how we reach the mind. We create a world for them here in which they can succeed, and they can go from it into the outside world. They are sent to us from many places."

"We keep them only till the age of twelve," Miss Goodspeed continued, "and then we send them into the normal world. A few stay with us. They work in the kitchen or on the farm."

Florilla followed Miss Goodspeed down corridors, up wide flights of steps, through dormitories, rows of iron beds under murals of fairy tales, into an infirmary ward and back outside through flower and vegetable gardens, blackened by frost.

"The frosts were late this year," Miss Goodspeed said, glancing at the plants with a practiced eye. The gardens were fenced neatly and practically laid out. The farm was equally tidy; even the brown-and-white cows in the barn had looked clean. All the buildings were of brick, carefully designed, unlike the accidental collections of sheds and lean-tos that Florilla remembered from the Pinelands farms, or the string of outbuildings attached in ramshackle procession to the farmhouses of New England. The farmyard itself was paved with fieldstone and had, at its center, a huge iron grating.

"That," Miss Goodspeed said, "is part of a revolutionary drainage system. Dr. Goddard was an amateur engineer."

Miss Goodspeed led her through the creamery, whitewashed, floored with scrubbed flagstones. Huge crocks were filled with cooling milk and cream. Two older girls were churning butter. They stood up awkwardly at Miss Goodspeed's entrance.

"Good morning, girls," she said. "Continue working."

As they walked back to the main building, Miss Goodspeed began to speak. At first, Florilla tried to answer but soon realized that she was not being addressed. Miss Goodspeed was delivering a monologue on the past and future of the Hinton School, on its founder, Dr. Goddard, who had studied with Dr. Seguin, himself the student of the famed Dr. Itard, in Paris. Did Florilla know about the wild boy of Aveyron? If not, Miss Goodspeed would tell her later. She, who had been Dr. Goddard's student, was clearly devoted to his memory. She was also growing old and feared that there would be no one to take her place. Girls came to her from the surrounding farms, usually those not sharp or ambitious enough to go into the local mills. They had little education. They worked for a time and then married. There was no one else to carry on Dr. Goddard's work. She stopped abruptly and looked hard at Florilla..

"I don't know why," she said, "certainly your arrival was peculiar, but I feel that you can help me. I feel almost as though you have been sent."

"But you don't know me," Florilla protested. "You know nothing about me."

"Dr. Goddard," Miss Goodspeed said, "taught me a great many things about the makeup of all human creatures, not just the feeble-minded. He had a supernatural understanding of people. He could see what the rest of us cannot. He believed that everyone had such sensory powers but that few could use them. I believe that you can." She paused. "Well, never mind. It's just a feeling that's all. Probably foolish. You're very young."

They walked on. The day had grown dull and still, the sky heavy.

"It could be snow," Miss Goodspeed said, "and it's very cold. I would gladly offer you hospitality for the night. You could stay in my cottage. Your animals are safe in the barn."

Approaching the main building, seeing the bleak hills behind it, Florilla felt a numbing desire to stop, to halt here, to sleep in a real bed, to return to an ordered place beyond the chaos of the world, a place like Benderville.

By the time they reached the first laurel bushes, the snow had begun to fall.

"You must stay now," Miss Goodspeed said.

Miss Goodspeed had work to do in the office, so Florilla went alone to the cottage. It was separated from the lawns of the school itself by a stand of firs. The snow blew in Florilla's face as she pulled the hood of her cape up over her nose and squinted her eyes against it. As soon as she turned to open the gate in the white picket fence, she turned out of the wind and entered a stillness into which the snow fell gently. She could make out the garden path by the remains of an annual border and ahead the cottage, white frame, carpenter Gothic, its frets and curlicues like decorations of the snow itself.

The hallway, with its single fanlight, was dark and cold with pegs for outer clothes and a scent of lavender. Hanging up her cloak, she realized that the only coats hung there were a man's frock coat and a heavy dark cape. As her eyes adjusted to the dimness, she noticed the top hats on the shelf above. Florilla found this singular. She hung up her own things, took off gloves and boots, and opened the nearest door.

No lamps had been lit in the room she entered, but large windows and a fire burning in the fireplace gave sufficient light despite the haze of snow. Above the fireplace hung a portrait that she recognized from the bust in the office as Dr. Goddard. She stood by the fire for a time, warming herself and watching the snow fall until she felt a presence at her back. She turned, an apology on her lips, believing that she must have blundered into a study where someone was at work.

There was no one else in the room, although it seemed that someone had just risen from the heavy mahogany desk in the corner, pushed back the chair, and gone perhaps to the window to look out at the snow. Curious, Florilla went to look at the papers neatly stacked on the desk. The top few were letters signed by Augustus Goddard. Beneath them were more papers in the same hand, each headed with a name and an age: histories of his patients. The inkwell was full, and the pen seemed to have just been set down.

Wandering further, Florilla looked at the books in the shelves: books on law, on engineering, many books in French. On the walls, in the spaces between the bookshelves, were engravings of Dr. Itard and his pupil Dr. Seguin, a few scenes of classical ruins, and a small drawing of Daphne, her arms branching into leaf.

"The wild boy of Aveyron," Miss Goodspeed began, "was Dr. Itard's most famous pupil."

She and Florilla sat at opposite ends of the table in the cottage's dining room.

"The boy was found in the woods, living like an animal. To Dr. Itard he personified human limitations. After all, the children you have seen today are merely a more obvious example of what we all face. They cannot escape their limitations, the limitations that have been placed on them. We, in turn, cannot escape our limitations, even though we have limited ourselves. We merely have the illusion that we can."

She paused for Florilla to absorb this truth and then continued:

"Dr. Goddard used to say that he preferred the feebleminded, because you could help them to use all the potential they possessed, something impossible to do with most normal people."

The force of Miss Goodspeed's devotion was compelling, and yet Florilla felt all the time, playing at the edges of her consciousness, someone in the room.

"Did Dr. Goddard live in this house?" she asked.

A blush rose in Miss Goodspeed's waxy cheek.

"Yes," she said. "As director this was his house. Now it is mine. You must be tired. Would you like to go to bed?"

Florilla was happy enough to agree to this abrupt dismissal.

Miss Goodspeed carefully placed the screen in front of the fireplace, blew out the candles in their tin holders, and picked up the oil lamp from the table. Florilla followed her from the warmth of the dining room into the cold hallway and up the stairs. Miss Goodspeed left her at the bedroom door.

"Goodnight, my dear," she said. "Millie will have made up the fire and left you a light."

This indeed was true. There was a fire in the fireplace, and an oil lamp stood on the table beside the four-poster bed, its circle of light falling on a leatherbound book stamped in gold: *Augustus Goddard, Diary Notes on Education*. It seemed there was nowhere in the house without reference to the man and his work.

Exhausted, Florilla sank happily into the comfort of linen sheets and heavy blankets. She slept at once and dreamed of the Pines, of sitting beside the Wading River under the cedars, hearing the birds: the cardinal's song, the blue jay's screech.

When she woke the next morning, the sound of birds had not ceased. She sat up. Could there be such birdsong in a New England winter? And the screeching was louder than any jay's. When Millie came to make up the fire, Florilla asked her.

"Them's Dr. Goddard's birds, miss," she said, hurrying away.

"Yes," Miss Goodspeed said at breakfast. "Dr. Goddard felt that there was much to be learned from birds."

Florilla thought that Dr. Goddard seemed to have found a lot to be learned from everything on earth. If he had stubbed his toe on a boulder, he would have taken the boulder home to learn from it.

"Birds like parrots," Miss Goodspeed continued, "imitate. So do children."

The aviary was in the attic of the cottage, a large space with a number of windows. One of Dr. Goddard's feats of engineering had provided heating sufficient for the lories and parrots that bloomed like uncanny flowers against the snowy landscape. A wood stove ran a copper boiler that forced heat through pipes around the room. It was tropically warm.

"The boy loved the birds," Miss Goodspeed said, "and he could imitate their calls. Dr. Goddard would take him to the aviary every morning."

"The boy?"

"Yes. The boy who was found by a neighboring farmer at the trough with his pigs one morning. Our own wild boy, grunting like an animal and naked as the day he was born. It was extraordinary. Dr. Goddard followed Dr. Itard's principles in teaching him. It's all there in his diary. I beg you to read it."

After breakfast, Miss Goodspeed took Florilla into the library and unlocked the drawer where the manuscript was kept.

"That is another likeness of Dr. Goddard," she said of the portrait above the fireplace.

"If you don't mind," she said, "I'll have Millie bring the parrot in. He was Dr. Goddard's favorite, and he does thrive on company. I'm away at the school so much of the day, and he makes Millie and Cook feel queer."

"Why does a parrot make them feel queer?"

"I don't know," Miss Goodspeed said. "They say he stares at them and talks in Dr. Goddard's voice."

The parrot, an African gray, was duly placed on his stand in the corner of the room, whence it watched Florilla with bright, intent eyes but remained silent.

Florilla had returned to the desk when, suddenly, the parrot spoke.

"Out of the woods," it said, "one summer afternoon as I was planting the vegetable garden."

Florilla stared at it. Could it be? Was that Dr. Goddard's voice?

"Dr. Goddard?" she ventured.

The parrot remained silent.

"I have been to the barn," Miss Goodspeed said that evening. "I perceive that the legend on the side of your gypsy wagon reads 'Jack Munion, Wizard of the Pines.' I also discovered within it many articles of the magician's trade and a handbill advertising the powers of the beautiful Rosemalia. You are she?"

"You went through my belongings?"

Miss Goodspeed ignored this.

"I believe, then, that you are a medium and that you can help me."

Florilla said nothing.

"Because, my dear, it is desperately important to me. I must communicate with Dr. Goddard, my dear Augustus, and I feel that you are the link, the catalyst."

"He's dead," Florilla said, "and, as nearly as I can tell, his soul is in that parrot."

Miss Goodspeed gave a little cry.

"You mean that you think his soul could have taken possession of the bird? Could he speak through the parrot?"

"Possibly," Florilla said, "though I've never encountered such a thing."

Miss Goodspeed's voice was agitated, and she peered so closely at the parrot that it drew up its wings and gave a loud squawk.

"Augustus," Miss Goodspeed cried, "is it really you?"

When the parrot did not respond, she turned back to Florilla.

"If I could talk to him, he could tell me what to do. How to go forward. You can make him talk to me. You can reach him, I know you can. All that paraphernalia in the wagon. You're a table tapper, aren't you? That's what you do!"

"No," Florilla said, "no. I traveled with a magician, but I do healing. I do not make contact with the dead."

Miss Goodspeed took her hands.

"But you *could*, my dear. You could do it. Just imagine. It would make your name. You'd be famous! *The story of the wild boy of the Connecticut Valley as told to Miss Flora Homer from the spirit world.* Oh, Dr, Goddard was most interested in all of that, in psychic powers. He experimented with some of the children at the school. He felt that the lack of intellect might mean that they were more closely in touch with the psyche. He had some very interesting results described in the notes I will give you to read."

Florilla tried to protest, but Miss Goodspeed was underway again.

"Of course," she said, "he hated frauds, and he felt that most of the mediums who did public work were frauds. But I know his spirit is still here with me at Hinton. Surely it must have drawn you here. He knew I needed help so that his work would not die, so that Hinton would remain a beneficent experiment. He was terrified that, after his death, it would become simply a prison for lunatics."

"What happened," Florilla said, "to the wild boy?

Miss Goodspeed's face closed; she looked away.

"It was sad," she said.

22

Snow was still falling on the morning of the second day. She was, Florilla realized, stuck in a shrine to the memory of Dr. Augustus Goddard within the grounds of the Hinton School for the Feebleminded.

"You see," Miss Goodspeed said, "it is still snowing heavily. There is no possible way for you to travel today. I must leave you, but I hope you will continue with the story of our wild boy."

Reluctantly, Florilla returned to the library. A fire crackled in the fireplace, and a pot of coffee and a plate of biscuits were set on the desk. Her life here was to be comfortable. Already she could feel the embrace of the institution, protective and constricting. Not so very different from Benderville.

She turned away from the desk and walked to the windows. Through the falling snow, she saw the school draft horses pulling the heavy stone roller along the road, keeping access open to the greater world. The harness bells rang; the boys in charge called to each other. And the snow went on falling. Florilla returned to the desk and opened the drawer.

The manuscript, titled *The Wild Boy of the Connecticut Valley*, was in the form of a diary in Dr. Goddard's tidy, italic script. Florilla opened to the first page.

"I was working in the vegetable garden that August morning when Nelson brought him to me. He found him feeding in his pig trough. He was naked, matted hair, filthy, grunting. He was fighting the pigs away from the trough, Nelson said, he almost seemed to speak their language. That struck me. I had always thought that if we could teach feebleminded children our language, then why not animals? Many birds learn not only the words but their sense."

She looked up at the portrait of Dr, Goddard, the beak nose, the gray crest of hair, bright, avian eyes in an otherwise reserved face. Was this someone she wanted to live with until the spring set her free? She supposed there were worse alternatives. She had food and lodging. The animals were safe and well cared for. Small chance that Munion would find her here.

The parrot watched Florilla read. Every time she looked up, the bird was staring at her. Whenever her attention wandered for any length of time, the parrot would screech.

"Romulus!" it shrieked. "My wild boy! I postulate!"

As she became immersed in Dr. Goddard's obsessive world, it made her think of Colin and the orchids. As Dr. Goddard catalogued his observations of the child, Florilla found herself transported to marshy hummocks or mossy clearings, seeing Colin on his knees, bent reverently over a blossoming *arethusa*.

"The boy," Dr. Goddard wrote, "can follow a track in the woods as well as any hound. At first, Nelson and I went out with him in the morning, and he would track game, trembling at the thickets where the pheasants hid as much as any dog. We thought he followed track, broken twigs, prints, indented grass. To test this, last night Nelson and I took him out after coon. He never once looked at the ground but slipped through the night woods inhaling great drafts of air, stopping sometimes, and turning in all directions, as if scenting the breeze. He stopped under a maple tree, and when we looked up, we saw a raccoon in its branches. The raccoon snarled and the boy snarled back."

A day later, the snow stopped but the drifts froze solid. Itinerants died on the roads. Local people came to the school for food. In the main schoolroom, the older children filled the proffered sacks with beans and corn and flour. Miss Goodspeed was gratified at the sight of the normal world coming to Hinton for help.

"And one day," she murmured, "so it may be throughout the world."

"Because you see," she said to Florilla later, "the psychic powers of these children, and others like them, may one day be more important than the cerebral powers of normal people. Dr. Goddard hoped and believed that. 'And a little child shall lead them.'"

"They are, after all...", and here she turned those fierce gray eyes on Florilla, "and always will be, little children. This place was Dr. Goddard's life, his dream. That is why it must continue."

As the days passed and the weather didn't abate, Florilla felt a kind of lethargy overcome her. Here it was comfortable and safe, a room of her own, food to eat. Here Munion would never think to look for her. Here, under the eyes of the portrait and in the presence of the parrot, was safety, even calm, like being in a boat on a windless sea. Each day she trudged to the barn to visit the animals, seeing that they were well cared for.

Dr. Goddard's manuscript detailed his daily efforts to teach the boy, using techniques derived from his work with the other children. He was a true son of the Enlightenment, believing that language and empathy distinguished the civilized being from the savage. And these were what he tried to teach the wild boy.

As Florilla read, the parrot watched her closely. Sometimes it spoke. "Letters," it cried, "make words."

Dr. Goddard produced wooden blocks with letters on them but found that the boy just stared.

Dr. Goddard's ideas, Florilla discovered, were taken from the work of Jean Itard, the French doctor, and his work with that other wild boy in Aveyron, France. She recognized the name on the spine of one of the leather-bound French books: *"De l'education d'un homme sauvage ou premiers devloppements physique et moraux du jeune sauvage de l'Aveyron."*

"I feel at times," Dr. Goddard had written, "that Dr. Itard has somehow sent this boy to me, that I may build on and establish his work. It is also a gift that Dr. Seguin, his pupil, is working here in this country. It seems that much in the stars is aligned."

But what had it been like for the boy? Had he been happier alone in the wild?

The answer came with a key in the back of one of the desk drawers. One day, when Florilla pulled the drawer out far enough, she found it, a small souvenir box inscribed *New York City Industrial Exhibition of All Nations.* Curious, she tried the other desk drawers. Three of them opened easily; the fourth was locked. The key opened it. Inside was a sheaf of papers. Florilla took them out.

The first folder held newspaper clippings.

The Wild Boy Found Groveling in a Pig Trough, Now Eats with Knife and Fork

Some stories mentioned Dr. Itard and the wild boy of Aveyron. Many quoted Dr. Seguin, who quoted Dr. Itard. From the diary, Florilla already knew that Dr. Seguin had come from New York to Hinton to see the boy and to test him.

Some of the clippings were announcements of appearances. "Dr. Goddard and the Wild Boy" in Hartford, in Boston, even in Lowell and Franklinville. There were also handbills and posters, some with drawings of a boy, naked on all fours, next to one of the same boy in jacket and knickerbockers.

Come and See the Wild Boy of Connecticut
The Transformation of a Savage

In the "before" pictures, the boy looked grotesque, worse than a wild animal. In the "after" pictures, he looked almost normal.

Florilla looked up at the portrait of Dr. Goddard.

"The boy!" squawked the parrot. "The boy!"

"The boy," Florilla said. "You exploited him."

The parrot ruffled its feathers and looked away.

Florilla laid the handbills out on the desk.

The parrot was silent.

The door opened. Miss Goodspeed stood in the doorway.

"That girl," yelled the parrot. "She did it! Did it!"

Miss Goodspeed saw the flyers on the desk.

"How did you find those?" she said.

"I found the key," Florilla replied. "Dr. Goddard made a showpiece of the boy, didn't he?"

"The world," screamed the parrot, "the world will know him."

"Stop," Miss Goodspeed cried.

The parrot made a faint creaking noise.

"It was for the school," Miss Goodspeed said. "For Hinton. We needed the money. Augustus would not have done it otherwise."

"You said the end was sad."

Miss Goodspeed turned away.

"He could have stayed here. He couldn't learn enough to live in the outside world. He didn't have to run away. And not in the city."

"Which city?"

"Boston. We tried for months to find him."

After a silence, Florilla said:

"He must have hated those shows."

"But Dr. Goddard was so good to him. So kind."

"No one," Florilla said, "wants to be put on exhibition." As she spoke, she saw her father and Dr. Pargiter, the lights, the desperate audience, felt her guilt at the exchange of money.

"If you would help me," Miss Goodspeed said, "to contact Dr. Goddard, perhaps he has found the boy."

"I told you," Florilla said. "I don't contact the dead."

"Through the bird," Miss Goodspeed said, "I'm sure you could do it through the bird."

Florilla sighed.

"I don't think so."

Miss Goodspeed's expression changed. After a brief silence, she said quietly:

"You ran away too. 'Jack Munion, Wizard of the Pines.' I imagine he'd like to know where you are, Rosemalia. But I don't think you want him to find you."

The parrot laughed and Florilla's scalp prickled with fear.

"If you don't stay here and help me, that might happen."

Miss Goodspeed pressed her hands together.

"It's not in my nature to threaten but I have little recourse."

Florilla did not reply.

As soon as the snow melts, she thought, as she lay in bed that night, *I must go. Somehow, I must go.* She would have to leave the animals— the hen, the rabbit, the doves, and the horse, but there was no way she could escape with them. Here they would be safe. She thought about the boy and pitied him. Even if it was for a better cause, Dr. Goddard had used him as her father had used her.

23

Florilla walked to Coverdale. She left the cottage in the middle of the night by the back staircase. She hated to leave the animals. She wished for the caravan, for the comfort of the doves and the hen and the rabbit, the companionship of the horse. But if she had taken the caravan, she would have been easy to track. Although there were stage routes down the valley, she couldn't risk anything so public. Instead, she stayed on the rutted, muddy road, ducking into the woods whenever she heard horses or wagons.

Coverdale was not much of a town. The Coverdale Mill was one long, low frame building set on the banks of a river in a narrow valley. The houses on the opposite side of the street were brick-faced stone, set hard against the hillside, so that their back yards sloped steeply up.

She reached the town as the first mill bell was ringing. The factory doors were already open. She watched the workers issue from their houses, a motley group, different from the tidy stream of girls in Franklinville, more like the immigrant workers of Lowell, whole families: men, women, and numbers of children. They gave her strange looks as she fell in with them, though she tried to smile. When she reached the doors, she asked the overseer about work in the weave room. He stared at her.

"You don't live here," he said.

"No," Florilla replied, "I just arrived."

He looked at her again.

"We don't get girls coming here," he said matter-of-factly, "but I'm sure there's work. Go down to the end door there and talk to the paymaster."

Thus began Florilla's days in the Coverdale Mill. The mill wove a coarse kind of plain cotton, so the work was not difficult. She found lodgings in one of the houses set against the hill. Each house was divided into rented rooms, so there could be as many as three families to a shared kitchen. There were only two families in the house where she boarded, having been taken in by a widow with three children. The woman was French Canadian, and she was glad for the extra money. She and her three girls, aged eight, eleven, and fourteen, all worked in the mill. The youngest was a bobbin doffer; the others tended looms.

"You'll have to sleep with me," the widow Laval said. "The girls have the other room."

The room she showed Florilla was very small and dark. It had only two windows at the back, so that after the winter sun had dropped behind the hill, there was no light at all. The only furniture was an old wardrobe, its cheap veneer peeling, and a rope bed.

"I have another bed out behind," the widow said.

Looking through the dirt-streaked panes of the window, Florilla did indeed see a bed under a lean-to amid the crusty patches of snow.

The bed, iron and somewhat rusted, was duly brought in and set up in the narrow room with some quilts and blankets retrieved from the bottom of the wardrobe. Florilla knew that she could have done worse. The widow and her daughters strove with the housekeeping during the hours they were not in the mill. The two rooms were clean, save for the dirt of years ground into the walls and woodwork. They washed the insides of the windows, but the outside panes were grimed over.

"The corporation says they will clean the windows," the widow said, sighing, "but never they do it."

The kitchen, shared with the other occupants of the house, an Irish family with five young, doughy-faced children, was filthy.

"I give up," the Widow Laval said to Florilla in her hoarse voice. "I try for a while to keep it clean, but with them it is impossible. One time— one time," she struggled for breath recalling the enormity of it, "they had a peeg in the kitchen. A peeg! I had to go to the corporation. They make them put it outside, but they don't understand anything wrong with it, oh no! Now they never speak to me."

The Widow Laval kept her few pots and dishes separate on a shelf in the girls' bedroom. In the same room was a small table where the family ate. The O'Keefes ate in the kitchen, the youngest child crawling under the table in search of scraps from the filthy floor. The only clean thing seemed to be the brass crucifix on the wall, which was regularly polished by one of the children. The black iron stove smoked continually. The walls with their faded, rose-patterned paper, were streaked with soot and grease; the stone sink seemed always to be full of cold, greasy water. There was little conversation among the O'Keefes. They stared at Florilla whenever she went into the kitchen. She did not know how to approach them. All of them, save the youngest child, who was only three, worked in the mill. This child was left, with several others, in the care of a mumbling, deaf old woman several houses away.

Working in the Coverdale Mill was not a happy experience. Florilla hated to see girls of fourteen tending looms, a job they got by virtue of their greater manual dexterity, while boys of the same age did the dirty jobs in the picking shed and carding room.

The mill owner seemed little removed from his laborers. He lived in a bigger house some distance from the center of the village, but it was in no way a mansion, merely a large farmhouse. He himself showed no guiding intelligence, simply a cunning that removed him from the mill floor. He worked in the counting room most days and was constantly around casting a calculating eye on all operations.

The weave room was dark with too few lamps, so the strain on the eyes was severe. Often, when she came out in the evening, Florilla's vision would be blurred. The eldest of the Widow Laval's girls, Marie Claire, suffered from terrible headaches. She would cry at night on returning from the mill. Though Florilla had wanted no one to know of her healing, after the first few nights, she went to Marie Claire's bedside and laid her hands on the aching head. In moments, the headache was gone, and the Widow Laval was crossing herself and muttering prayers in French.

"Please," Florilla said, "I will gladly help Marie Claire and all of you, but I really don't want anyone else to know about it."

"But of course," the Widow Laval said. "Of course, my dear."

She told Florilla her whole life story after that, how she had come from Canada with her husband who had found work in a nearby town. When he was killed in an accident, she was left with the three children, no money, and no relatives.

"So, I had to earn my living, and they tell me about the mill, so I come here to Coverdale."

"Would you like to go back to Canada?"

The Widow Laval shrugged.

"What is there for me in Canada with no husband? Here I have work, and the children have work. We can live."

"They don't go to school?"

The widow shook her head.

"School is in the next town. They couldn't work and go there part of the day."

The middle child, Jeanne, was obviously clever, and so Florilla began giving her lessons in the evening when they came home from the mill. She was eager to learn but often so tired that she would fall asleep over whatever book Florilla had scrounged from the library in the next town. Florilla began to teach them all on Sundays after church, to read, to write, and to cipher a little.

The months passed, spring came, and June brought wild roses to the scrubby hillsides. Heat hung in the low, swampy valley. The weave room was mercilessly hot, the windows nailed shut to preserve the humidity that kept the threads from breaking. It was so hot that Florilla often felt sleepy and lightheaded. Sometimes the rumble of the looms became a distant thunder in her dreams, till Mr. Cantwell, the overseer, shook her roughly awake. One hot June day, the sound of the looms rose to a crescendo and became a thin high whine, and she saw swarming clouds of black, although what composed them she could not make out.

"Hi, Florilla," the woman next to her hissed, "look sharp. Mr. Cantwell's coming."

Florilla bent to her loom with a sense of foreboding.

It was two days later, coming out of the mill, that she recognized her waking dream. The air was thick with mosquitoes. Dogs raced maddened down the street, and everyone ran for home. By the time she got inside, Florilla's arms and face were covered with welts. The O'Keefe children wailed in the kitchen.

In that year, malaria was epidemic. When the youngest Laval girl came down with it, Florilla nursed her through it. A week or so later, Florilla felt lightheaded standing by her looms. She thought it was the heat. She was moving to ask her bobbin doffer a question when the room began to sway and darken. She was aware of the sweat trickling down her back before she fainted.

She was carried home and put in the widow's own bed. The world moved in and out of darkness. Widow Laval crossed herself and wept.

The fever grew worse. In her delirium, Florilla traveled through realms of heat and cold. Sometimes she walked through tropical jungles where parrots, like those at Woodland Place, shrieked incessantly, and vines brushed her face, something like the vines in the gardens at Benderville but covered with giant, fleshy flowers in red and purple and a luminous, ghostly white. Sometimes she wandered through snow, high amid jagged mountains. Although her feet were bare, and she wore only a cotton shift, the cold was incidental. It came only in gusts with the mountain wind. And here, too, there were flowers, tall plants, looking like *habenaria* but with huge flower spikes of a greenish, phosphorescent white. She tried to pick them for Colin, but they screamed like mandrakes when she broke the stems.

Colin was finding the green heat of the rain forest stifling. His clothes clung to his body, and rivulets of sweat ran down the back of his neck. Far above him in the branches of the dead cream nut tree, he could see the dependent clusters of a *paphinia* orchid. The flowers were huge, perhaps eight inches across, dark reddish brown, in clusters of half a dozen. He was sure it was *Paphinia grandiflora,* and he had to have it. Dr. Cutler had been trying for two weeks to train a pet monkey to go up the tree and bring down the blossoms, but so far the monkey had only succeeded in destroying a perfect cluster of *Cattleya violacea.* So the native bearers had tied ropes to the tree and were in the process, with laments and curses, of felling it.

"Come along, men," Dr. Cutler yelled at them while Dr. Boothroyd made frantic calculations of the angles of fall.

"Don't, for God's sake," Colin cried, "let them have it fall on the orchids!"

"Don't worry, boy, don't worry," muttered Dr. Boothroyd.

The wood creaked and groaned till at last the huge tree fell with a crash and Colin dove at once among the branches. The *paphinia* was safe. The other botanists gathered round.

"It is the *grandiflora*," Colin said. "A perfect specimen."

"By Jove," breathed Dr. Cutler.

Now, Colin thought, if it could just be packed carefully. They carried sphagnum moss with them for the purpose, moss he had gathered in the pine barrens, and as he lifted the epiphytic plant from its home to place it in the box full of sphagnum, he thought of Florilla. Her face appeared before him, as it so often did. He dashed the sweat out of his eyes, and the image was gone. The orchids remained, and they were beautiful.

24

The message took a week to reach Benderville. When Benjamin Bender took up the envelope addressed to him in an unfamiliar hand, he wondered if it could be from the young man, the botanist, if perhaps he had found Florilla. But the writing was much too uneducated for that. Nor was it Munion's. When he opened the letter, the handwriting inside was hardly legible. It took him several minutes to puzzle it out.

> *Dear Sir,*
>
> *We have found yr name in the paprs of Flora Homer a girl working here in the mill she is Very bad with the malarial fever and may not Live.*
>
> *Signed,*
> *Mrs. Audette Laval*
> *Coverdale, Coneticut*

Benjamin Bender sprang from his chair, pulling frantically on the bell rope. He met Lethe as she came gliding down the hall.

"Lethe," he cried, "have them saddle my horse right away and bring a second horse, bring Vulcan!"

"Quickly," he shouted after her. "It's Florilla, she's ill. Tell Ananda to pack me a change of clothes."

Lethe ran to the stable yard. In minutes, the horses were at the door and, a short time later, Benjamin Bender was strapping the saddle roll onto the back of the saddle. He had dispatched the stable boy to fetch Andrew McKenzie and Thomas Fitzgerald.

"Quick, boy!" he said. "Tell them to run."

The boy tore off down the street, his feet sending up spurts of white sand. He came back with the dye master panting behind him and ran on to the company store.

"I am going to Connecticut," Benjamin Bender said when both men stood before him. "I shall be gone at least a week. I can be reached at this address.

He handed them a piece of paper on which he had written:

Mrs. Audette Laval
Coverdale, Connecticut

"Just keep things running as they are."

He swung up into the saddle, took the reins of the other horse and galloped off across the bridge and down the road that led to the west.

The two men stared at each other. Benjamin Bender had never done anything so impulsive before.

"It's Miss Florilla," Lethe said from the veranda.

Benjamin Bender found the old white mule and the hybrid wagon tied to a tree in Crowleytown. Bursting into the shanty where Dr. Peace was treating a child, Benjamin Bender explained his errand. Dr. Peace left medicine for the child, and Benjamin Bender paid one of the older boys in the family to drive the mule and cart to Benderville.

"Malaria," Dr. Peace muttered, pulling numbers of cigar boxes out from under the wagon seat and sorting the contents as Benjamin Bender waited impatiently with the horses.

"Ah," Dr. Peace said, "I've got it. Thank the Lord."

They left the horses at a livery stable at Mount and took the stage north. From there, without stopping for sleep, it was a two-day trip by rail and stage. Early on the third day they made Putnam, Connecticut, where Benjamin Bender managed to commandeer a farm wagon to drive them on to Coverdale. The sky was swollen with thunderclouds.

"Do you know a Mrs. Laval?" Benjamin Bender asked.

The farmer shook his head.

"Sounds like a Canuck. Coverdale ain't big. Somebody'll tell you.

"Fever's been bad over there," he added after a silence.

The mill bell was ringing as they reached Coverdale. Though the trees were in full leaf, and wildflowers grew in the ragged grass along the road, the town, in its narrow valley, had an unkempt bleakness that greatly upset Benjamin Bender.

"Working in the mill," Dr. Peace said as they got down from the cart.

"So I suppose."

"These low rivers," Dr. Peace shook his head. "Worse than with us."

The two stood on the main street as the workers passed curiously around them. They were a poor looking lot. Benjamin Bender reached out and caught a woman by the arm.

"Madam," he said, "excuse me, but I am looking for the Widow Laval."

She pulled her arm away but pointed at the houses across the street.

Florilla was delirious. She shivered so that the bed shook, even though every covering in the house was piled over her. She could not escape the cold wind. Strange, bright flowers grew amid the branches of the familiar pines. Then she was walking through a field of lilies. The ground grew stony, painful to her feet. She clambered over rocks.

"My God," Colin cried. "There it is in that cleft—and look at the color!"

The Indian guide stared impassively into the distance as Colin climbed the rocks while the rest of the party gathered brush to make a fire for tea.

They were now in the highlands, and the air was very cold, "China or India?" Dr. Boothroyd inquired. "Damn difficult to do anything with these bloody gloves on."

He and Dr. Cutler, in knitted hats, huddled gnomishly by the fire.

But Colin, impervious to the cold wind from the peaks above had reached his destination and was carefully culling an orchid of pale frilled blooms, a *cattleya*, but one unknown in Europe.

The Widow Laval was crying.

"These last two days I have stay with her," she sobbed. "My Marie Claire minds my looms."

Benjamin Bender looked down at Florilla's face, the skin startlingly white against the gray sheets, the golden hair matted. He listened to the thin shallow breathing.

Dr. Peace knelt beside the bed and pulled the covers back.

Benjamin Bender turned away as the doctor began taking the boxes out of his bag. He went into the other room where he found Madame Laval still crying.

"Please, madame," he said carefully accenting the French, "don't trouble yourself so. You've done the best you could do. It is in God's hands. Now, pray, is there somewhere nearby where you could get some food and more blankets?"

"Only the company store. I will go there."

Benjamin Bender dug in his pocket.

"Here," he said, handing her several dollars. "Spend all of this, please, and bring back some nourishing food, and blankets if you can find them."

All night, Dr. Peace sat by the bedside. In the squalid kitchen, he had ground and mixed his herbs, watched with a mixture of awe and terror by the O'Keefes, and managed to get Florilla to swallow them. She was only aware, in her dreaming, of confused voices, far away, like echoes. But by morning her fever had broken, and she returned from those foreign landscapes to the dingy little room. At first, the dark face of Dr. Peace swam among fronds of vegetation, the flickering parrots. She thought him some Amazonian native, and fought against a paralyzing weakness and a thickened tongue.

"How far is it to get back," she whispered. "I can't find the road."

"Florilla," Dr. Peace said gently, "you've been very ill, but we're here now."

Other faces swam into focus: the widow, Marie Claire, Jeanne, Benjamin Bender. The scene was somehow far less real than the orchid-infested fever dreams.

"I don't understand," she said weakly and could feel tears squeezing from the corners of her eyes, partly from the terrible weakness and partly because, amid that strange flora, she had hoped she might find Colin.

Benderville

1856-1857

25

Florilla lay once again in her own bed in her own room in the mansion at Benderville. For days, she woke only fitfully from periods of sleep that were blank and without dreams. She knew where she was, but the summer days came and went outside the window. For a time, she knew only light and shadow and the dim lamp that burned all night to light Lethe's silent appearance at her bedside with tumblers of bitter liquid for her to drink.

Gradually, different pieces of the world came back to her. One day the air was filled with birdsong; on another, the smell of the woods, of ferns and pine needles in the hot sun filled the room. On another, she noticed the shadows of the wild cherry branches on the wall, the vase of flowers that Ananda replenished every day: roses, pinks, phlox, campanula. She stared at the colors: white, blue, pink, and yellow misting before her eyes. One by one, it seemed, her senses were returning.

Dr. Peace came most days, and Benjamin Bender came morning and evening. He never spoke, simply sat by the bed for a time reading. She was glad for his presence though too tired to speak. She was glad for Lethe carrying her in strong arms to the chair while Ananda changed the sheets. And for Ananda clucking as she brought in soups and drinks. She was the only one who really talked, and she went on rattling and scolding as she always had.

"Chile, chile," went her litany, "why did you go and leave us? You nearly die out there."

"Out there" was the world beyond Benderville, to Ananda a place of constant danger.

During the hours that she lay in bed, Florilla wondered how she could be where she was, back at Benderville. At first it seemed no less strange than the dreams of flowers and mountain peaks. Often, Lethe gliding in her white nightdress seemed the shimmering fragment of a dream. She wondered how she had come there. No one talked of it. She remembered Coverdale, even the day she had fallen ill. But only when the Widow Laval finally came to see her, twisting her handkerchief and blurting the whole story of her illness, of Benjamin Bender's kindness, of the cottage in the village, so clean with a garden (oh, the vegetables she could grow, the apple trees there already), of the girls in school at last, even Marie Claire, did she understand everything.

Slowly, Florilla's strength returned. At first, she got up for several hours to sit in a chair; then she went outside to lie on a bench in the shade of the black walnut tree. There, in the peace of the garden, it seemed that the shards of her life reassembled. If she tried to remember in sequence what had happened from the day that she ran away from Benderville, she could not. But as she lay watching the shade move, the bees buzzing in the hollyhocks, memories came back to her, as fleeting as the shadows of birds and clouds on the grass, but so intense that they were like waking dreams. She would find herself in the rose garden at Woodland Place, examining an *arethusa* orchid with Colin, posing for Boffin as he painted Daphne, then trapped at Sim Place, and on the journey to New England. She saw the Blackstar Mills blaze in an October sunset, the streets of Lowell and Boston in winter. She saw inn rooms and boarding house rooms and hotel rooms, a succession of anonymous places. She saw Hinton and the pictures of the wild boy. She saw Miss Goodspeed, Munion, Dr. Pargiter, the mill girls, the families of the Paddy camps, the pale, ill children of Coverdale.

Benjamin Bender continued to sit with her in the late afternoons. Ananda would bring benne wafers and the China tea that had been specially sent from Philadelphia. He never really asked her any questions. He brought her books and talked to her about the mill, comparing Benderville to the loathsome conditions of Coverdale.

"The machines," he would say, "are only as good as the people who run them. It has been proven that those well housed and fed do better work. We noticed that in my early days at Franklinville."

One afternoon, Benjamin Bender put down his cup of tea and cleared his throat. It was a hot August afternoon, and the garden seemed to be filled with hummingbirds and golden light. He looked over at Florilla. Though her face was still thin, and the brown shadows lingered under her eyes, he could see the old Florilla returning. She hadn't the ethereal, translucent look that had so frightened him in the early days of her convalescence. He thought it safe now to speak.

"My dear, after you left us, sometime after last autumn, I had a visit from a young man named Colin Drysdale, the nephew of Lord Amberwell at Woodland Place."

As he watched, he saw a flush come into her cheeks, her lips parted slightly. There was an eagerness in the blue eyes that he hadn't seen since her return from Coverdale. It smote him, for he had so little to give her, but he continued.

"He was looking for you. Apparently, he is a botanist and came home from a botanical field trip to find you missing—it was his idea that you might have gone looking for orchids at Sim Place."

"Yes," Florilla said slowly, "yes, I did. The *habenaria*. I still have it, in my carpet bag. I'd like to give it to him."

Benjamin Bender pressed on.

"He seemed very fond of you," he said. "I gather you were to stay on at Woodland Place as governess for the Amberwell children?"

"Yes," Florilla said.

"Of course, we none of us knew where to find you then, but I thought perhaps now you should try to be in touch with him—or I should."

Florilla looked away, watching a butterfly swaying on a tall stem of phlox.

"No," she said, "I didn't intend to stay there. I went to Sim Place to get the orchid, but had my father not found me there, I only meant to go back to Woodland Place to leave the orchid for Colin. Then I would have left myself. For Philadelphia perhaps."

"But why?" Benjamin Bender asked. "I gathered from the young man and from that rather irritating German woman who came to look at the mill, that you were very happy there."

"I was," Florilla said, "for a time. Colin Drysdale was my friend. But he will be back in England now. He is engaged to be married to an English girl."

"I had no inkling of that," Benjamin Bender said in surprise. "Are you sure?"

Florilla smiled.

"Yes," she said. "It is necessary. He has a beautiful old house, and she is an heiress."

"He said nothing of that to me."

"Nor to me. Lady Amberwell told me after he had gone away."

Benjamin Bender was puzzled but said no more.

Dr. Peace visited regularly, bringing herbal remedies to increase Florilla's strength. Others came to see her. Mr. Magreavey the schoolmaster brought her a book on the Jersey Devil that he had newly acquired and which he thought might interest her.

"There's been a sighting," he said seriously, sitting beside her on the veranda taking tea. "Over in the Plains. A collier there was sleeping in his clearing when he was woken up by what he thought was a wind-storm—then he saw the shadow of it, right over him, it picked up a pig he was keeping and carried it right off into the swamp. He ran straight out of those woods to the Speedwell Tavern, I can tell you."

Mr. Magreavey sipped his tea.

"They say he's out of his head the best part of the time now," he mused. "Like the fiddler over at Quaker Bridge who heard the Air Tune one night. Trying to remember it made him mad."

Another afternoon, Fiona came. She had married Tom Matthews and carried with her a baby of three months. She seemed to have grown taller, her figure rounded, fuller.

"Well, Florrie," she said, "what a time you've had."

She fussed a lot with the baby and described in detail the cottage were they lived as though it were unique, when Florilla knew that the interiors of all the cottages were just the same. Fiona didn't stay long because the baby was fractious and left saying:

"You must come to supper when you're stronger."

Even Andrew McKenzie arrived one afternoon. He was stiff and polite and gazed at her when he thought she wasn't looking. Florilla watched him curiously. Fiona had told her that he had become some-thing of a recluse, and she was sorry in a detached way, but she couldn't find much to say to him.

She was happiest when Jeanne, the middle Laval girl, came to sit with her in the garden and talk with excitement of the books she was reading. She was filling out, her face was no longer pinched, and there was a bloom in her cheeks.

26

One morning in early October, Florilla rose early. She ate breakfast in the kitchen and then walked down through the garden carrying the lunch Ananda had packed for her. The spicy scent of chrysanthemums mingled with the tang of the wild grapes tangled in the hedge along the canal. A heavy dew had picked out the spider webs between the heads of the asters in the herbaceous border. Wasps, still numb with the early morning cold, were beginning to crawl over the windfall pears. She went through the trellised gate and crossed the footbridge over the still black water of the canal. Here the smell of the grapes was so winey and strong that she stopped to pick a few.

The mules were being hitched for the trip to Benderville Landing when she reached the stable yard. The men all nodded to her and called out, "Good morning." One of Fiona's brothers fetched for her the little sorrel pony and trap. He helped her up.

"Be careful now," he said. "Stay on the roads."

The pony snorted and tossed her head in the pleasure of the cool morning. The mill bell was just ringing as they crossed the bridge onto the road. Ducks rose from the mill race, their wings breaking the surface of the water, leaving a diamond spray that seemed to hang in the air.

On the veranda, Benjamin Bender looked at his gold watch before waving good-bye to the pony and trap. He sighed, looked down Main Street to where the parade of hurrying workers was just beginning, looked back at the sand road bending into the trees where trap and girl would soon vanish. In Franklinville, he thought, the maples on Indian Top would be turning already, while here his maples still held their heavy green leaves. He thought of Florilla in Franklinville, in all those other towns. How futile his attempt to save her had been, how futile it still was. What was she searching for at a deserted Woodland Place? What would she find?

He heard the gate latch click. Andrew McKenzie stood at the foot of the steps in his dye-spattered clothes, as though he, like the trees, was changing with the autumn. In his big, stained hands he held strands of roving. A new dye, Benjamin Bender thought. He remembered the Blackstar gingham, the weaving of the colors.

"Well, McKenzie," he said heartily, "a new dye?"

"You shouldn't have let her go alone," Andrew McKenzie said in a rasping breath as though the words hurt him.

"Man, man," Benjamin Bender said, "she left us long ago."

Florilla drove to Woodland Place. For several weeks she had thought about it. She would not have gone except that Benjamin Bender had told her the Amberwells had been posted to Rome. That meant, she assumed, that the place would be closed up. Since that discovery, the desire to see it one more time had possessed her.

Despite the ambiguity of her errand, she felt her heart rise at being back here in this familiar landscape, the white sand road beneath the pony's feet. She passed through towns—hamlets really—with their bleached frame houses and barns, occasional sawmills and general stores. One stretch of road crossed cranberry bogs.

At midday, she reached the turning to Woodland Place. She pulled up for a moment and hesitated before she turned the pony onto the road.

The gates across the drive stood open. Surprised, Florilla drove through. Between the oaks, she could see one wing of the house, the sun glimmering on the French windows of the sitting room. The driveway swept ahead to the clump of rhododendrons. The pony's hooves crunched on the oyster shell. They passed the rose garden and Florilla glimpsed the pale pink flowers of late-blooming shrub roses.

Clearly, the house was closed. Shutters were fastened over most of the windows. Florilla got down from the trap. Everything was still except for the pony's stamping at flies, the occasional bird trills. Feeling like a character in a fairy tale, Florilla took the reins and led the pony down the drive between the house and the outbuildings, planning to tie her in a shed, away from the sun and flies.

As she passed beneath the tower, one of its casement windows was thrown open, and, looking up, she saw Freeman Jade.

"Flora!" he cried. "Stop! Wait! Is it really you or a trick of this halcyon light? Don't go in any case! I am descending."

And descend he did in great haste.

"Flora! Flora!" he repeated, embracing her. "Is it really you?"

He looked just the same, and she felt as though, at any minute, they might all gather round her: Miss Euphemia Potts, Dr. Alcock, Boffin, Mariana Fleming.

"Dear, dear," Freeman Jade said, "you do look a bit older, paler and thinner. More serious perhaps. How long is it?"

"A year," Florilla said.

Freeman Jade clicked his tongue.

"Many events," he said.

"Are you alone here?"

"Not entirely. You remember Mrs. Davis, the cook? She and her husband and daughter, they're living in the kitchen wing, though they went to Atsion this morning. The rest of the house is shut up as you can see. I just exist in splendid solitude in my little tower, oversee things—you know."

Florilla nodded.

Freeman Jade was clearly delighted by the advent of another civilized being and was in a mood to talk. They tied the pony in the shed and took Ananda's ample picnic onto the terrace. Florilla gazed down the sweeping lawn with its skirtings of laurel, to the brown river and the dock where she had first arrived.

"The Amberwells were posted to Rome last spring," Freeman Jade was saying, "and the major part of the household departed with them. The children went, of course, and are reported to be enjoying school in England. I gather they go back and forth between the two countries."

"And Boffin?"

"Boffin is back in London, happily ensconced in the more Bohemian reaches of Chelsea. The good Frau Muehlberg is back in her native land, naturally."

"And Miss Fleming?"

"In New York, being a blue stocking, and I believe Alcock had a symphony played in Philadelphia. But what of you, Flora, you who left us so cruelly? Young Colin was nearly out of his mind when he came back and found you gone."

He looked at her with his head on one side.

"You are an artful one, Flora. It was only through our dear and peripatetic Frau M that we learned of your connection to Benderville. Colin went there looking for you. Brought Lord Amberwell's best horse home lame.

"Quite a scene," he added with satisfaction, cutting another piece of Ananda's Virginia ham. "He came back saying that you had been kidnapped by your own father—a wizard, I believe—and taken with him to be a part of his act. An extraordinary tale, is it true?"

"Yes," Florilla said. "It is. We toured New England until he disappeared, and I ran away."

Briefly, she told him of Hinton, of Coverdale, of the malaria and her return to Benderville.

"Good heavens," Freeman Jade said, "the stuff of fiction surely. And meanwhile young Colin set out for South America. The orchids you know. A trip to collect specimens."

Florilla remembered with sudden sharpness the strange fever dreams of mountain peaks and jungles, and those exotic, fleshy flowers. Colin had been there.

"Is he there now?" she asked carefully.

"I'm really not sure. He was going back to England by some circuitous route. He might be anywhere. What marvelous ham this is!"

Sitting there, Florilla felt a great loneliness sweep over her. She realized that she was waiting for Colin, for his step on the terrace, his voice from the lawn, his canoe bumping into the dock. But nothing disturbed the silence save the cultured hum of Freeman Jade's voice.

"I shall be writing to Lady Amberwell this week," he said. "I shall tell her that I've seen you and that you are well. She was most upset and blamed herself when you left."

"I wouldn't have left like that, without a word," Florilla said. "Tell her that I hope she is well and the children."

"Of course, of course. I understand."

The afternoon turned cold, and as Florilla drove away down the drive, a sharp wind made the oak leaves murmur. She pulled the pony up at the gates and looked back at the house, ghostly beyond the trees. Then she drove on, stopping only once near to rest the pony and stretch her legs. In the moss by the side of the road, she found the curly grass fern. She stared at it for a while, and then, kneeling down, carefully uprooted it.

27

"I must be meant to heal," Florilla said to Benjamin Bender. "It's a gift I must use."

They were at dinner on a late November evening. A huge fire burned in the marble fireplace at the end of the long room. The pine logs snapped and popped, shot out sparks like summer's fireflies. Outside, a wind was blowing from the east, rattling the shutters and lashing the bare branches of the maples against each other.

"But my dear—" he began.

Florilla was determined. She had thought a lot during her convalescence about how to manage what she saw as the rest of her life. The future stretched interminably: she had to name it, shape it, give it order.

"I thought," she said, "that perhaps I could have one of the cottages, that I could work in the mills part-time for rent, and I could heal. People would come to me."

For a brief moment, Benjamin Bender imagined the ragtag assortment hobbling into his tidy world. He swallowed it, but Florilla seemed to have read his thoughts.

"Only the mild cases would come here," she said, "I would also go out through the Pines, if you could let me have the pony and trap. There are many who would otherwise never hear of me. Sometimes I could go with Dr. Peace, and I can learn a lot from Indian Mary."

Lethe came in with a platter of vegetables. Candlelight glowed on the polished surfaces of wood, china, and silver, the curves of the fruit centerpiece. Benjamin Bender took more carrots.

"What about all your learning," he said.

Florilla gazed at him down the table.

"Isn't that what learning is for? To deepen whatever natural gifts one has or allow one to recognize them?"

He couldn't answer, looking at the pale, beautiful, serious face and remembering the disheveled child the first day he had seen her. Who would have imagined?

"All right, my dear," he said, as Lethe began to clear the plates. "There is a cottage vacant at the end of the village since the Larkin family moved on. You can have that."

Florilla moved into the Larkin cottage, though she continued to take dinner at the mansion with Benjamin Bender. He also decreed that she could not go back to work in the cloth room until the next autumn when he felt her strength would be truly restored.

Florilla was happy in the cottage. Its floor plan was the same as in all the others: one room downstairs, whitewashed with dark woodwork, a shallow brick fireplace, a built-in cupboard, a door at the back that led into a kitchen ell with its sloping roof and a black iron stove. Another door in the main room opened onto steep stairs that led up to the bedroom, a large room with sloping eaves and windows on both sides, one looking onto Main Street, the other toward the woods. There was also a small front porch, on which, in fine weather, one could sit surrounded by a neat, fenced garden. Even in November, it was cozy.

A scolding Ananda, who didn't see the sense of it, helped her load dishes, sheets, and blankets into a wheelbarrow to trundle down the main street. With familiar things, like the quilt from her bed at the big house, the cottage became home.

Benjamin Bender gave Florilla the pony and trap for her own use. She spent some weeks with Indian Mary learning about the uses of plants.

They would go into the woods, even into December, finding hips and haws, seeds and barks to be powdered or infused. There was much joy for Florilla in such practical learning, and soon she began to make forays into the surrounding Pines. At first, some were suspicious of her because she was said to be the granddaughter of the witch. However, she soon became known for her healing, and people began to make their way to her door.

Benjamin Bender worried about her long absences riding around the countryside. He worried about the colliers in the woods, the denizens of the hamlets, and even the return of Munion. However, she had to do something, he knew. He brooded on the young man, Colin Drysdale, and his visit. It still puzzled him.

One day in March, another strange young man arrived on foot at Benderville. He entered the company store in midafternoon, when no one was about save Thomas Fitzgerald taking inventory, and asked for Flora or Rosemalia in a strange accent.

"Don't know who you mean," Thomas Fitzgerald said, staring at him.

The young man was not daunted.

"The Healer of the Pines," he said dramatically. "that's who I want to see."

"Oh," said Thomas Fitzgerald, "you mean Florilla Munion. You better speak to Mr. Bender. You can go on up to the house and wait for him."

"Thank you," said the young man, "I will do that."

The young man's name was Rupert Cavendish. He was an English social reformer making a tour of America. He was also a friend of the Amberwells and of Freeman Jade. He had made a stop at Woodland Place, and it was there, by the most extraordinary of coincidences, he had discovered Florilla. Well, not discovered her exactly. He had heard of her from another friend who shared his interest in psychic phenomena as they pertained to utopian experiments. Visiting the mills in New England, this friend had heard tales of an amazing young woman.

The young woman was traveling with a very ordinary magician and some sort of phrenologist. In the act, she was called Rosemalia, but she was the real thing, a healer who helped the mill girls. He had wanted to find her, had followed the posters to Boston, but there the trail had gone cold.

"And there I was," he said, "telling Freeman, and suddenly he was telling me that this Rosemalia was really a girl called Florilla who had grown up here, Mr. Bender. Imagine my surprise, for I knew of you and your social and industrial experiment here at Benderville."

"Fascinating," he continued, "the juxtaposition of false and real magic—an image fitting man's plight and his institutions. We of the Utopian Society believe we are all healers, though few of us at present are able to use our powers. If we can only heal ourselves, we can heal society. We are most interested in the powers your ward possesses."

"Go on," Benjamin Bender said.

"We have some very influential backers. Very well off. We could provide passage to England for the young lady, if she would agree to lecture and spend some time training our members."

"You'll have to ask her," Benjamin Bender said.

"Right," the young man said, "I'll do that. Where will I find her?"

"She's healing over near Shamong today. She should be back at dusk. I suggest you stay for dinner and the night. I have, as you see, plenty of room."

Rupert Cavendish smiled.

"Thank you," he said. "By the way, Mr. Bender, we are also very interested in your theories on the industrial community. Many of us have read Irmgard Muehlberg's description of her visit here."

"No," Florilla said. "Really, I have made my life here, and people depend on me. I can't leave to lecture in a strange country. I cannot even explain the healing I do, much less train others to do it."

Rupert Cavendish was disappointed. He strode back and forth in front of the fireplace in the mansion's drawing room. He seemed as comfortable in the house as if he had always lived in it. Florilla supposed that a country of houses like Amaryllis Court would give one a certain ease. He would feel no awe at Benderville's mansion; it would seem quite an ordinary house to him.

Benjamin Bender sat in an armchair near the fire. Florilla sat close by. He watched the fire give color to her pale, tired face. He found that he hoped she would agree but thought it unlikely.

"I must go home," Florilla said, "it's late."

"I will walk with you," Rupert Cavendish said, turning to Benjamin Bender, "if that's all right by you, sir."

Benjamin Bender nodded.

As Florilla and Rupert Cavendish walked down the street together, a light snow was beginning to fall. Near the mill, they passed the watchman swinging his lantern.

"It's quite amazing," Rupert Cavendish said, "what Mr. Bender has created here. I have been to New Lanark, and though this derives from the theories of Robert Owen, New Lanark has little of its warmth and beauty.

"You should see England, Miss Florilla," he added as he left her at the gate.

Florilla was glad to be inside the familiar little cottage. She poked up the fire, pulled the screen across, and left the door to the stairway open so the heat could rise.

Colin got the letter in Para, Brazil. His party had emerged from the jungle the day before and gone straight to sleep in the comfort of the Queen Of Para Hotel. Actually, it was all Colin could do to sleep, for, in the Wardian glass case, the unknown orchid bloomed. He sat in the half dark and contemplated its pale pearly petals, the lavender striated sepals. If only it could withstand the journey.

The next day, they went to the British Consulate to make arrangements for the journey home and collect any letters. Colin had one from his brother Algernon.

"Good God," Colin said. "My father has died."

"Well, well," Dr. Boothroyd said, "we stand before the new Lord Fenhope."

"Oh, God," Colin said.

For now, he knew, Amaryllis Court was truly and finally in his hands. His were the reins to take up. He would have missed the funeral, the burial in the family crypt in the village church. Algernon would have been there, impeccable, reliable, and longing to be Lord Fenhope. Colin once again cursed inwardly the accident of birth that had made him the elder. He walked out onto the balcony with its vista of palm trees and crowded streets and, in the distance, the mountains with their crystalline snow peaks. Back to England, to the small hills and valleys, to Amaryllis Court, to Sophronia. Sophronia's mincingly pretty face swam before his eyes, her dark curls, the mole near the corner of her mouth that was pronounced bewitching. It filled him with a feeling much like revulsion. Suddenly, as though she were standing beside him, he saw Florilla's face, her profile, the mass of golden hair as he had seen it so many times while they bent together to study a specimen. She overwhelmed him. He crumpled the letter in his hand and called her name.

"Now, my boy," said the consul, who was somewhat deaf. "Don't take on. Knew your father well. Time for him to go."

The snow turned to sleet and beat against the windows. Florilla awoke with a start. But it was not the sleet she heard, nor the wind in the pines; it was a voice calling her name, and the voice was Colin's. She sprang from the bed and ran to the window. She could see little but a swirling vapor that dimmed the moon. She felt weak again and slightly dizzy, as though the whirling snow had entered her head.

"Colin," she whispered and knew that somewhere he had called her, that she must go to England. She felt that she could almost be carried there now on the icy, rushing wind.

Florilla left two weeks later for an indefinite stay in England. In her trunk, she packed these things: Colin's press, the *habenaria,* and the curly grass fern she had found in October on the road to Woodland Place.

England

Spring 1857

28

Florilla sat on a wrought iron bench in the garden heart of a Kensington square, alone on the April morning. She gazed at the tidy beds of primroses and daffodils. They seemed to be blooming everywhere. She had been in England two weeks, most of it in London, a guest in the tall, cream-colored house she now faced, the headquarters of the Utopian Society. There she had met with members of the British Healers Association. She had traveled with them to meetings and healing sessions all over the city, and sometimes by carriage into the surrounding countryside, to manor houses in small villages where keen amateur interest in the society's ideals was evidenced.

She had decided to go alone that afternoon to an exhibition at the Royal Academy of Art at Burlington House. Boffin had talked about exhibiting there, and if she could find Boffin, he might have news of Colin. She was half afraid now that the sound of his voice in the night at Benderville had come at the moment of his marriage to Sophronia Scrubdale. If, at such moments, one's life rushed before one's eyes, as she thought it might, he would have thought of her.

She found her way to Burlington House easily enough, crossed the courtyard hung with banners, and made her way up the long flight of steps to the gallery. At the top of the steps she halted in confusion, for she faced *Going West*, the painting of herself and Colin painted that day at Alice Furnace. She moved closer. Several people were standing in front of the painting.

"Yes," she heard one of them say, "it was painted in America while he was out there. Actually, young Lord Fenhope posed for the frontiersman."

"Pretty girl," someone else said.

"Yes," drawled the first speaker. "Don't know who she is."

Florilla pulled her cloak up around her face and moved quickly into one of the other rooms. She looked around at the paintings, mostly large canvases of biblical and historical subjects, a number of portraits, among which she recognized another painting by Boffin of the Amberwell children. She did not see Boffin himself, though she knew it was silly to think that she would. Instead, she bought the catalogue which listed the names and addresses of all the exhibitors and set off to find him.

She rang the bell at the address in Tite Street. The bell hung beside a wooden gate to a large house set in a walled garden. As its rattling echoes died away, the gate was opened by a young girl dressed in biblical costume.

"Excuse me," Florilla said, "but I'm looking for Mr. Hunt."

"Come in then," the girl said indifferently, "he's painting in his studio."

The garden Florilla entered could hardly be called a garden, being a cross between a paddock and a junk yard. A white goat, followed by her kid, skipped nimbly over several large casts of Corinthian capitals. Another plaster cast of Laocoon wrestling the serpents stood near the path. A rope tied round one of the serpent's heads was attached by the other to a plane tree making a clothesline hung with a strange assortment of garments, male and female. Weather-beaten pieces of furniture and lumps of marble and granite stood among overgrown flowerbeds.

The girl led her into the front hall and pointed up the stairs. Florilla went up. There were several doorways on the first two landings, but they stood open on scenes of domestic chaos and seemed to be bedrooms. She had climbed to the very top of the house when she heard voices from behind a double door. She knocked.

"Come in!"

The voice was unmistakably Boffin's. Florilla opened the door.

He stood with his back to her, and she was aware of a complicated scene on the dais in front of him. A man, in the dress of a Roman centurion, was kneeling at the feet of a tall woman semi-dressed in an animal skin, her wild red hair flying out around her face.

"Boffin," Florilla said.

Boffin turned and dropped his palette.

"Flora!" he cried. "But how ever did you come here?"

The centurion and the maiden gazed sideways, trying to hold their pose.

"That's all right," Boffin called to them. "I have it. You can take half an hour."

"Time for tea," sighed the girl and went to put a battered kettle on the hob.

Boffin, meanwhile, was hugging Florilla in disbelief.

"But you know," he said, "you've just missed Lady Amberwell. She was here to take the children out of school. She told me that she had had a letter from Freeman Jade saying that you were back at Benderville, and now here you are in London!"

He turned to the girl who stood warming her half naked body in front of the fire. The centurion had left the room.

"Make us some tea, Lizzie, there's a good girl."

"I am," Lizzie said in a strong Cockney accent. "Basil's gone to get some bread to toast."

"The thing is," Boffin said as they drank tea and ate Lizzie's toast, "you really must meet some of my friends, the Pre-Raphaelite Brotherhood. They all wanted to paint you after they saw *Going West*. But what are you doing here?"

Florilla did her best to explain.

"Healing," Boffin said. "Magic and spells. Didn't Colin tell me your father was a wizard?"

"A magician," Florilla said. "He has no special powers."

In the early evening, Boffin walked her back to Kensington. He took her arm.

"I'd like you to pose for me again, Flora, I'd like to paint you as Ariadne."

"Boffin," she said, "where is Colin?"

"Damn," Boffin said. "You never will forget him for a moment. You should know, I suppose, that he is now Lord Fenhope and has married Sophronia Scrubdale. It was announced in the papers some weeks ago."

"Then he came back from South America."

"Yes. Recently, the paper said."

Boffin took her by the shoulders.

"Now listen, Flora or Florilla. It is too late. And, anyway, what would you want with Colin really? Do you want to sit down in the country in a great leaking barn of a place while he's off somewhere squinting at plants? You're an artist, Flora, you need other artists."

"All I want to know," Florilla said stubbornly, "is that he's all right."

Boffin laughed.

"He's all right, that one. He'll always be all right."

But, as he said it, he remembered Colin's return from New England to Woodland Place, the pain and anger, the long search. It did not, however, suit Boffin to tell Florilla this. It did not suit him for several reasons. One was vanity. He wanted Florilla for himself as a model, and felt heartbreak was a weakened state to play on. Although his natural kindness might have subverted this, he was dependent on Lady Amberwell's patronage and he knew how Lord and Lady Amberwell would react to anything that blocked the forthcoming marriage of Colin and Sophronia.

"He has great plans for Amaryllis Court, you know. Going to make it one of the botanical showplaces of Europe. Brought back all these orchids from South America. Cranking up the greenhouses and whatnot."

Florilla said nothing, but her head was filling with the strange blossoms of her dreams.

29

The next morning, Florilla left the house in Kensington very early, taking to the streets of London as once she had taken to the New Jersey woods. She walked for a long time with no specific aim except to head north, away from Chelsea, Boffin, and his associates.

After a time, the imposing shops and churches and other public buildings gave way to streets of row houses, then to warehouses and tracts of scrubby open land, sometimes disciplined into a sort of common, sometimes used as a general dumping ground for domestic and manufacturing effluvia. One street was all depositories, huge temples decorated with plaster caryatids; another ran along the railroad yards; in yet another were the stables for dray horses and the omnibus sheds. She passed a red brick brewery, stone garlanded, which filled the air with the pungency of malt and hops. At the next corner, she hesitated, wondering if she had gone far enough, if she shouldn't turn back now and return to Kensington. Walking had achieved its purpose; she was too weary for thought. As she looked about, her eye was caught by a distant glittering like water catching the sun. But surely there was no water nearby. She was a long way from the Thames. An ornamental lake or pond in some nearby park seemed unlikely in this semi-industrial district.

A dray loaded with barrels came out of the brewer's yard, heavy horses going at a spanking trot, its huge wheels splashing mud on her skirt. The lad driving shouted something she couldn't hear, though she could make out laughter above the sound of hooves striking on cobblestone.

Florilla crossed the intersection and walked on, the glimmering still visible in the interstices of the shabby, terraced houses at the end of the road. She realized that she was not seeing the glitter of water but of glass. Beyond a narrow street called Glover Terrace, rose an immense glass structure. Rounding the corner, she saw that it was the first of three greenhouses built in the Gothic style, like glass churches. Painted on each of them was the legend:

REGINA AND PARADISE NURSERIES

HOLLOWAY

LONDON

IMPORTERS OF EXOTICS

Orchids, Florilla thought. She crossed the pavement, went up to the first of the greenhouses, and peered through ogee arched windows that could have graced a Venetian palace. What she saw were orchids, hundreds and hundreds of them. They grew in baskets and on small logs suspended from the roof; they grew in pots on rows and rows of benches. Drawn by their extraordinary, dreamlike shapes and colors, Florilla opened the door and entered.

At once she had exchanged the raw English day for a pleasantly tropical warmth. She stared into the strange, particolored faces of *cattleyas*, *masdevallias*, *laelias* and *stanhopeas*, breathing their breath of gardenia, menthol, and cinnamon. She saw them, infinite in number and variety, voluptuous and foreign compared to the fragile, subtle orchids of the Pines. She had not imagined them like this, but she had dreamed them so. Here in this glass temple to their beauty and strangeness, she wandered bemused. Their colors stunned her: pure white, palest rose, deep magenta, crimson, yellow, tiger-striped and leopard-spotted, leaves like the leaves of lilies, leaves like grass, tendril roots feeding on air alone. Staring up at a brilliant *Laelia purpurata*, she almost ran straight into an old man in a linen smock who was making a careful pencil drawing.

"I beg your pardon, madam," he said. "Can I be of service?"

"Oh no," Florilla said, "I was just passing. I am interested in orchids, as it happens. Go on with your drawing, please."

"I had really finished," the old man said. His eyes were very blue and his cheeks pink.

"Arthur Paradise at your service," he said. "I am always happy to meet a fellow orchid fancier. Now, tell me, which are your special favorites?"

"At present," Florilla said, "South American ones."

The old man smiled eagerly.

"Then the contents of this house will be familiar to you. But I wonder if you would like to see some fascinating specimens recently brought back for us from Brazil?"

He described an expedition financed by the Regina and Paradise Nurseries, stroking the glossy leaves of a huge *Grammatophyllum speciosum* all the while.

"I'd be most interested," Florilla said.

"You're American, I believe?"

"Yes," Florilla said.

"There is not, I understand, so much interest in the orchid with you in America as there is in England. You know a *cattleya* went at the sales rooms recently for three hundred pounds! But I've no doubt the interest will come. And, of course, as you know, there are native North American species. Young Lord Fenhope has done some interesting work there."

Young Lord Fenhope. Colin! These must be the very orchids he had hunted. Florilla caught her breath. She was almost trembling as Arthur Paradise led her down the long cathedral aisle and through a door in the back. They crossed a courtyard, Florilla drawing her cloak about her against the cold, and entered a tiny greenhouse.

"Quickly," Arthur Paradise cautioned her as he held the door. "We must beware of drafts."

In this greenhouse, there were about twenty plants hanging in baskets.

"Now these are all from the Cutler–Boothroyd expedition to Brazil, which I was mentioning to you just now. Here we have *Paphinia grandiflora.*" He pointed to a plant with large, dependent clusters of dark reddish brown flowers. "And here *Oncidium gardneri.*" He touched the graceful panicles of bright yellow flowers with brown mottled edges. "Then *Laelia perinii nivia, Oncidium forbesii, Laelia harpophylla.*" These last showed little in the way of bloom, and he paused to explain that due to their long sea voyage, many would not bloom for a time.

"But now," he said, "I will show you my treasure, my jewel among many jewels. Here, my dear, look here."

The plant in question, suspended from the ceiling in a basket, bore amid the typical flat green leaves of the *cattleya,* a spike of frilled buds of a nacreous pallor.

"*Cattleya fenhopiana,*" the old man breathed. "Discovered in the Brazilian highlands by Lord Fenhope."

He gazed at it with reverence.

"An entirely new species," he murmured.

Florilla stared at Colin's orchid.

"The young Lord Fenhope who recently married?" she asked.

Arthur Paradise gave a start.

"Not yet!" he cried. "My dear, not yet. We still have five days for the *fenhopiana* to come into full flower. We are breathless with anticipation."

"Can't he marry till it blooms?" Florilla thought this quite possible.

"No, not really. But we do hope to be able to put it in the bridal bouquet."

"You are making the bridal bouquet?"

"Of course. All the most glorious white orchids that we have in flower: *Rodriguezia fragrans, Phalaenopsis aphrodite.*"

Florilla stared at *Cattleya fenhopiana.*

"How do you transport them?"

"Very carefully, my dear," he replied. "By train on April twenty-eighth, the morning of the wedding. I shall take the bouquet myself."

"Is it a long way?"

"Just to Oxford and then about three miles by carriage to the house, to Amaryllis Court."

"Perhaps I shall see you on the train," Florilla said quickly. "I am planning to go to Oxford myself."

"Oh, I do hope so," Arthur Paradise said, "for then I could show you the *fenhopiana* in full flower. I shall be taking the eight thirty from Paddington."

Florilla barely noticed her surroundings as she walked back to Kensington. Wagons splashed her, a small boy ran into her, and she almost walked right into the side of an omnibus.

She was going to Oxford? Had she really said that? What did she think she was going to do? She could hardly steal him at the altar. And yet she felt lighter and happier than she had for days. *He wasn't married.* Not yet. Although she told herself he might as well be, somehow it felt different.

When she got back to her rooms at the Utopian Society's house, she settled herself on the wide window seat overlooking the square in the gentle light of the spring evening. After a little while, she went to her trunk and took out Colin's press, the *habenaria,* and the curly grass fern. Why had she brought them if she hadn't meant to see him?

She sighed. She would wait. After the wedding, she could send them to him. Perhaps they might even meet. That night, her dreams were troubled. In them, there was a man who looked like Colin but wasn't and a girl who looked like Fanny Greenough but wasn't Fanny Greenough. The two were walking hand in hand.

Boffin came round the next day to ask her to dinner with others of the Pre-Raphaelite brotherhood.

"I hear young Colin has gone to the Alps for his honeymoon," Boffin said smugly. "Probably making that poor girl scramble round after edelweiss, so to speak." He laughed.

Florilla gazed at him coolly and did not respond.

Florilla would never know how it happened that Rupert Cavendish would ask her to collect a book from a bookseller in Regent Street a day after she had stumbled upon the Regina and Paradise Nurseries.

Regent Street was the busiest shopping street in London. After collecting the book, she wandered past its shops, many the establishments of dressmakers, the grandest, Madame Denise, proclaimed herself "dressmaker to the court."

As Florilla gazed idly at Madame Denise's sign, wondering if it was the sort of place Lady Amberwell might patronize, the door was flung open and a young woman came rushing out, followed by an older woman in black who Florilla supposed to be Mme. Denise.

"Oh, please," she was saying. "Oh please, dear Miss Scrubdale, I'm sure the next fitting will suit you better."

Florilla froze.

The young woman turned, the hood of her cape fell back and Florilla saw a head of dark curls like Fanny Greenough's.

"No," the young woman said furiously, stamping her foot, "I *told* you what I wanted, and you utterly failed in the execution."

At that moment, a hansom cab drew up and a young man jumped out. For a dizzying moment, Florilla thought it was Colin. The same height, the same chestnut hair, but a stockier build. This must, she realized, be his brother, Algernon.

"Sophronia," the young man cried. "What's wrong?"

For Sophronia Scrubdale had burst into angry tears.

"Oh, Algernon," she sobbed, "it's all wrong. My wedding dress. It's all wrong."

"Please, Miss Scrubdale," Mme. Denise implored, hands twisting her pinafore. "It will be redone to suit!"

With Sophronia sobbing against his shoulder, Algernon Drysdale assured Mme. Denise that they would return in the morning. Then he ushered Sophronia Scrubdale into the waiting cab and gave the cabman an address. The cabman flourished his whip and they rattled away.

"*Merde!*" said Mme. Denise. She spat on the pavement and hurried back inside.

Florilla stood rooted to the spot. She had just seen Sophronia Scrubdale and Colin's younger brother, together on an errand that surely should have involved Colin. Now perhaps she understood the dream.

30

Florilla had no trouble finding Arthur Paradise on the Oxford platform. He was accompanied by two of his lads carrying a wicker hamper amply labeled FRAGILE. He was explaining to the guard that it was impossible to put his treasure into the van. The guard went away shaking his head.

"Good morning, Mr. Paradise," Florilla said.

"Ah," he replied eagerly, "the young American orchid fancier. I have it here. I have it here in bloom in the bouquet." He lowered his voice reverently. "*Cattleya fenhopiana.*"

"Do join us," he said of himself and the bouquet, having sent the lads off to a second-class carriage, "in our compartment. I have had to buy my orchids a seat." He gave a faint, wry mile.

As soon as they were underway, safely sealed in their compartment, Arthur Paradise drew back the lid of the hamper. He sighed.

"There, my dear. There it is."

The orchids lay on their bed of moss like fallen stars. She caught her breath at the *fenhopiana,* its fragile petals, blue tinged, its throat streaked with lavender.

"Is it not beautiful?" he said simply.

Florilla nodded.

"Will you deliver it to the house?" she asked.

"No, my dear, no. To the church. The less handling the better. The less picking up and putting down. No, it will be handed to the bride as she arrives at the church. I shan't open it again till then."

He was clearly too anxious about the orchids to ask Florilla where she was going or anything else about her presence on the train. At each station stop he waved his hands vigorously at any passengers approaching the door, shaking his head vehemently to announce that the carriage was full.

"Drafts. Pipe smokers," he muttered anxiously to Florilla.

The train rushed on through the countryside. The fields were green, and every clump of trees seemed to shelter the flash of bluebells. The sky was full of towering clouds, and the steam from the engine billowed past the windows. Mr. Paradise insisted on keeping these tightly closed lest any cinder be blown into the compartment. He became more agitated as they neared their destination and broke off the description of an expedition to Moulmein he had made in his youth.

"Where is Amaryllis Court?" Florilla asked as the train began to slow for the station.

"Mudslake," Mr. Paradise said, "Lower Mudslake. I must just find the guard. Keep an eye on my beauties."

He jumped up and went out into the corridor, leaving Florilla alone with the bouquet. She bit her lip at the audacity of her plan, hesitated for a moment, then lifted the lid of the wicker hamper. Opening her own reticule, she unwrapped from its tissue paper the slender stalk of *habenaria* and stuck it carefully in the center of the bouquet, close to the unearthly transparency of the petals of *fenhopiana*.

At Oxford station, Arthur Paradise and his lads bundled the orchids into a waiting conveyance, a brougham marked Scrubdale & Son, and waved a flustered good-bye. It was early morning of market day in Oxford, and the streets were very crowded. Undaunted, Florilla, jostling amid the crowd, asked the way to Lower Mudslake and set out in the direction indicated. On the outskirts of North Oxford, she came to a signpost: Lower Mudslake, three miles. She set off at a brisk pace.

The countryside delighted her: gentle hills, fields sloping down to willow-guarded streams, elms and beeches of a girth she had never seen. Sheep grazed in the brilliant green depths of the grass. She passed a herd of red cows being driven to pasture by a small boy and a collie dog. It was glorious to be alone in this small-scale world, with its cloud-clotted sky, a world so entirely different from the tangled woods and stark spongs with their broken silvery trees. That landscape was eerie and wild, this gentle and domestic. After a mile or so, she heard hoofbeats behind her, the creaking of wheels, and soon a farmer's cart drew abreast.

"How far be ye goin'?" the farmer said in guttural accents.

"To Lower Mudslake."

"I be going that way," he said. "Come up then."

The horse, a fat bay cob, stood placidly as the farmer helped her up beside him.

"Do you know Amaryllis Court?" she asked after they had rolled along in silence for another mile.

"Ar," he said, which seemed to be an affirmative because he nodded with it.

"Is it on this road?"

"I'll show you," he said, "when we get to the village."

He looked at her curiously.

"Where be ye from?"

"America," Florilla said.

She might have said China without causing a reaction more amazed. He stared at her and said nothing more.

The village of Lower Mudslake was a crossroads with a few houses and a pub called The Rose And Thistle. Here the farmer let her down. He pointed with his whip down the right turning.

"Big 'ouse is down there," he said.

"Thank you," Florilla said and started off in that direction. This was a narrow road between fields with black iron fences which gave way after a time, on one side of the road, to a high stone wall. Florilla followed it until she reached iron gates at the mouth of a weedy gravel drive running down an avenue of elms. The drive dipped so that all she could see of the house were several stone chimneys against a hillside. She hesitated and saw that she was standing in the road between the park gates and the churchyard. The church itself was quite small, squarely Romanesque, and built of Cotswold stone, the churchyard filled with leaning, moss-covered slabs and yew trees. Florilla noticed that the door to the church stood open A little afraid to go down the driveway, Florilla took instead the pathway to the church door and stepped inside.

It took her eyes several minutes to adjust to the interior gloom, during which time she became aware of a certain amount of bustle around the altar. Pale morning light fell through the clear leaded panes of the altar window onto masses of flowers piled on the steps, in the choir stalls and on the altar itself. Various receptacles, urns, and bowls of silver and glass stood on the altar steps and the flagstone floor of the chancel. Women were arranging the flowers in these, while two young girls plaited ivy into long ropes.

No one noticed Florilla standing in the shadows at the back of the church. She looked around her at marble plaques set in the wall, memorials to Fenhopes and Drysdales stretching back to the time before the colonization of America, a time when only the Leni Lenape inhabited the Pines. The feeling was peaceful, as though there were a mesh, a web, something against which one could lean, something that would hold beyond the ephemeral human connections of one life. But, clearly, an ephemeral human connection was to be celebrated at St. Ursula's (for so the church was named) that afternoon.

"Let's get on with it, Jemima," she heard one of the women say. "We've got to get over to the house to help them."

"I think she's got a bit of a temper, Miss Sophronia," muttered the one called Jemima. "And she don't care tuppence for Lord Fenhope." Her companion ignored her but the girls plaiting the ivy giggled.

"I saw them," Jemima said sturdily. "Her and Mr. Algernon."

"You never!"

"I did. I saw them, hanging onto each other for dear life in the library when Lord Fenhope was out mucking about with his greenhouses."

A shocked silence erupted into shrieks of giggles.

"Well, I can understand," Jemima said, "who wants to come second to a bloody orchid?"

Florilla, still unseen, left the church. She crossed the road, and with the stealth of the wild, young Florilla, ran into the trees that bordered the drive to Amaryllis Court, a double row of elms, making their own narrow, grass carpeted alley. She slipped from tree to tree till the drive sloped down and she saw the house. Florilla stopped, drew in her breath in wonder.

In front of the house, the driveway crossed a stone bridge over an ornamental lake stocked with waterlilies and ended in a sweep of gravel surrounded by green lawns shaded by huge, dark, spreading trees. The house itself was, to Florilla's eyes, enormous, far bigger than the mansion at Benderville or any of the houses of the rich in Franklinville or Lowell or Boston, far bigger even than Woodland Place. The stone façade was severe, without pillars or verandas. As she watched, the sun came out from behind the clouds and the stone turned golden. She remembered the day at Long Branch when, looking out to sea, she had imagined that she saw Amaryllis Court in the golden clouds. And now here it was, the light softening the angular stone almost to the mistiness of clouds, as unreal as something in a fairy tale. She continued from tree to tree till she reached the lake. She couldn't cross by the bridge without making herself visible to the hundred eyes of windows. Luckily, the lake was bordered at one end by enough sprawling rhododendrons to provide cover.

There had begun to be some activity around the house, windows thrown open and gesticulating figures appearing in and out of doors. Florilla crouched in the rhododendrons. From this angle, she could see one wing of the greenhouses that stretched out behind the house, their panes of glass catching the morning sun in sheets of light.

As she watched, a figure emerged from this incandescence and she recognized Colin's familiar long stride. Her heart leapt in her throat. He was walking straight toward her, or straight toward the edge of the lake. He squatted on the bank, reached out to touch one of the water lilies, lost his balance and fell in.

"Blast!" Colin said.

The water was only knee-deep, and he took the opportunity to inspect a few more water lilies. Then he straightened up and looked meditatively across the lake to the sloping avenue and beyond it the park gates, and beyond that the church, where, in a matter of hours, he would be married. The familiar landscape dissolved before his eyes, replaced by the hummocks and marshes of the Pine Barrens. He thought of Florilla with the now familiar dull pain. He tried to turn his mind away from it, to the Amazonian orchids in the greenhouse that his future father-in-law had already refurbished as a wedding present. Instead, he seemed to see the small, delicate orchids of the Pines, the orchids of bog and field and wood.

"*Habenaria cristata*, rose pogonia, *Arethusa bulbosa*, helleborine, *Cypripedium acaule, Spiranthes gracilis*," he murmured, and with each name he saw Florilla's face at a different angle.

"*Habenaria integra*," he said finally, desperately, because with that came blankness and the image of the shanty at Sim Place. He had thought to exorcise her but somehow could not escape the feeling that she was near. It was very odd.

"Lord Fenhope! Milord!"

The cry came from the door of the house.

"Coming, Mrs. Pleasance!" Colin called back, and, with one last tender look at the water lilies, climbed the bank and squelched off across the lawn, stopping after a few steps to pour the water out of his shoes and continuing in stocking feet.

Florilla watched him go. She crept through the rhododendrons to the foot of the double avenue of elms and then she ran, no longer trying to hide herself. She was, in fact, passed by the vicar, bowling along in a dogcart, so busy constructing his homily that he noticed nothing.

Through the park gates and into the road Florilla ran. Her first impulse was to turn and run back down the road, all three miles back to Oxford, but from that direction came a carriage drawn at quite a clip by a pair of spanking bays. Florilla ran instead through the church gate in among the yews. It was as well that she had because she now recognized Lord and Lady Amberwell, Julian and Rosabel, as the carriage turned in at the park gates.

What if Colin didn't notice the *habenaria*? Or what if he did and it meant nothing to him? What had she done? All kinds of thoughts ran through Florilla's head. Would she give in, pose for Boffin, make some life for herself in the good-natured Bohemia he inhabited? Would she stay on with the Utopian Society in that pleasant house in Kensington? Surely either would allow her glimpses, from time to time, of Lord and Lady Fenhope? She heard a door open and, drawing back into the yews, saw Arthur Paradise emerge from the vestry door. He stood rubbing his hands together nervously, then drew out a large gold pocket watch and stared at it. She had to smile as he went back inside. That was where he must be guarding the bouquet, the *Cattleya fenhopiana* and the *habenaria*.

As the hour for the wedding approached, the church began to fill up while villagers arrived to stand at the churchyard wall. Florilla, seated quite comfortably on a stone monument to some early Drysdale and well hidden by the yews, watched. She saw Colin enter the church with the young man she had seen in Regent Street, his brother Algernon. The organ began to play a Bach fugue.

A carriage came down the road, drawn by a matched pair of chestnuts and gleaming with so many accoutrements that even the Amberwell carriage was put to shame. Florilla watched transfixed as a small, stout man, bald-headed and red of face, descended. He looked so like the Lowell mill owners of those evenings with her father that she almost laughed aloud. Reaching the ground, he turned to help the bride alight, for this was Mr. Erasmus Scrubdale. Garbed in white satin which Mme. Denise must have redone, veiled in antique lace, came the bride, Miss Sophronia Scrubdale. A liveried footman, who had leapt from the back of the carriage, hastily gathered up the train which he handed to the small page and bridesmaid who had descended with Sophronia. At the church door, Arthur Paradise bowed and presented the bouquet. Florilla caught only a glimpse of Sophronia Scrubdale's dark curls as the organ began a piece by Handel and the entourage moved into the church.

Colin waited at the altar with his brother Algernon. He knew the beginning of the Handel signaled the arrival of the bride, but he did not look
round, continuing to stare out of the altar window at some sheep in
a field. He made his mind as blank as was possible. He had given his
word; it must be got through somehow. He wished that he did not
keep hearing, somewhere in his head, Sophronia's silly giggle. He must
remember her dark eyes, her pretty ways. Although, in fact, he had
hardly seen her since his return. She seemed to be always in Yorkshire
or London. She almost seemed to be avoiding him. He supposed he
hadn't minded it, busy as he has been with the greenhouses.

The organ music swelled. He heard the rustling of her train and then
she stood beside him.

"Dearly beloved," the Vicar began.

Colin looked down at the bouquet Sophronia carried. He was anxious
to see the *cattleya* in flower again. How beautiful it was, trembling slightly
with the tremor of her hands as it had trembled in the mountain wind.
Idly, he went over in his mind the names of the other orchids: *Rodriguezia fragrans, Phalaenopsis aphrodite.* Suddenly he saw it. He blinked his
eyes, but it was there, small, in the center of all those white flowers.

"*Habenaria integra*," he breathed, the delicate Pine Barrens orchid
that Florilla promised to find for him. In a flash he understood what it
must mean and the cry broke from his throat.

"Florrie!"

He pushed past Algernon and ran down the side aisle of the church
into the spring sunshine.

"Florrie!" he cried. "Flora! Florilla! Where are you?"

Oh, what had she done? Florilla took a deep shaky breath.

"I'm here," she said in a small voice, "over here in the yew bushes."

Colin thrust his way through the dark branches, and they stood facing each other beside the stone monument to mortality in the everlasting gloom of the yews. He didn't ask her how she'd come there; she didn't ask him how he could be marrying Sophronia, they simply fell into each other's arms.

"Florrie, quick," Colin said.

He led her out of the yews, across the back of the churchyard and through a gate in the back wall. They were on a green track in a wood, a wood glimmering with the smooth, silver boles of beeches.

"They won't find us here," Colin said, for the organ had finally stopped playing and a commotion had broken out at the church.

"Look," Colin said, picking a primrose. "*Primula acaulis.* You don't have this growing wild in America."

"Colin," Florilla said, "you're supposed to be getting married!"

He looked at her, reached out and laid a hand on her head.

"To you," he said, "yes. But I think we'd better let them sort themselves out a bit."

"Oh," Florilla moaned, "I should never have done it."

Colin smiled.

"I'll show you something."

He led her back to the churchyard gate, a high wooden gate with a barred window set in it. She looked through. At the edge of the crowd, she saw the bride in the arms of Algernon.

"You see that's it," Colin said slowly. "I just didn't notice, I was so busy with the new greenhouses and everything. When I was away, she really fell in love with him. It's her parents who wanted the title and the house."

And so it was that Algernon married Sophronia Scrubdale two days later. The decorations in the church didn't even have to be changed.

After the first shock, Erasmus Scrubdale was quite happy to settle for the Hon. Mrs. Algernon Drysdale and someone he considered a solid son-in-law.

"All that botanizing," he said, "never could understand it. And now he's marrying the Amberwells' governess, and they tell me her father's a magician—an *American* magician."

Colin and Florilla were married in St. Ursula's in a very small, quiet way on a May afternoon. Afterward, they walked together down the drive to Amaryllis Court. A rain shower had just passed and the returning sun glowed from the warm stone. But neither would have noticed. The house could have been the shanty at Sim Place or a bush camp on the Amazon now that they were together.

"It won't be such a grand honeymoon," Colin said to her, "since Erasmus Scrubdale isn't paying, but I still want to go to the Alps to look for the *Chamorchis alpinea* and various gentians. I thought we'd stay in a little pension I know of. Very simple and comfortable."

Florilla thought of huge, snowy mountains, the mountains in her dreams.

"The wildflowers are beautiful in early summer," he continued. "Sophronia would have been such a bore—I'd have had to leave her at the hotel and come back to check on her amusement all the time. But you'll come with me, won't you Florrie? You'll climb the mountains and be my companion?"

"I will. Of course, I will."

"You might find some old mountaineer to heal," he said happily, patting her hand.

Florilla smiled.

31

The clash of the mill bell sent the songbirds wheeling into the air once more. Benjamin Bender stood under a fringe tree in full delicate bloom and reread Florilla's letter about her marriage to Colin Drysdale, now Lord Fenhope. He smiled and shook his head. How strange was circumstance.

When at last he looked up from the letter, he saw a figure on foot approaching down the road. As it drew closer, he recognized Munion the wizard.

Jack Munion stopped at the garden gate. He looked tired and travel-stained, and his voice, when he spoke was weary.

"All right, Bender," he said, "where is she?"

"Good morning, Mr. Munion," replied Benjamin Bender with exaggerated civility. "Are you inquiring about Florilla?"

"Yes," Jack Munion replied, "that one. Ran off with my horse, my wagon, my animals. I tracked her here."

"Well, I'm happy to say that she's not here now. She is in England, where she has just married the young Lord Fenhope."

Munion stared in amazement.

"You're a liar," he said.

"Not at all. Read this."

Munion took the letter. He read laboriously, moving his lips. Then he threw it on the ground, ripped the stained felt hat from his head and stamped on it, swearing.

"Really, Munion," Benjamin Bender said dryly, "that can't help."

"We could have had it all!" Munion cried. "Money, fame, the capitals of Europe— and she goes and marries some broke foreigner, all because you taught her that fancy stuff, Bender."

He reached up and picked a sprig of fringe blossom, snapped his fingers, and made it disappear.

"Gone like that," he said, "and me left poorer than I was before."

He turned to leave, turned back.

"If you want me, Bender, I'll be at Sim Place."

Benjamin Bender watched him go and then stood for a time gazing at the river. As he watched, a pair of wild swans dropped from the sky, skidded on the surface, and then swam gracefully, side by side, out of sight.

End Notes

Although all the characters and many of the places in the book are fictitious, some have their origins in real people and places. And a few real people mentioned in the story might need more explanation.

PEOPLE

Benjamin Bender

The inspiration for Benjamin Bender is Richard Harris. Richard Harris was one of three brothers who owned the Harrisville Mill in the Pines. Richard was the one who lived at Harrisville full time in the big house or "mansion." Harris had extensive gardens in which he grew plants from all over the country. A benevolent employer, he provided married workers with a rent-free house and one acre of land. Harrisville also had a company store, a school, and a horse-drawn ambulance service.

Dr. Peace

The character of Dr. Peace owes much to Dr. James Still (1812-1882), The Black Doctor of the Pines. The son of freed slaves, he was self-taught, learning much about herbal remedies from local Indians. Like Dr. Peace in the novel, Dr. Still traveled the Pines in his wagon, bringing comfort to isolated farms and towns. James Still's brother, William Still, was active in the Underground Railroad which we see in Lethe's nighttime forays.

Prosper Hunt, known as Boffin

Boffin is a member of the Pre-Raphaelite Brotherhood (founded 1848), a group of English painters, poets and art critics, including John Everett Millais, Edward Burne-Jones, and the painter/poet Dante Gabriel Rosetti. The Pre-Raphaelites sought a return to the detail, color, and composition of Quattrocento Italian art before what they saw as the corrupting influence of painters like Raphael.

Marianna Fleming

Marianna Fleming is loosely based on Boston blue stocking Margaret Fuller (1810-1850), activist, journalist, social reformer, and advocate for women's rights. Fuller traveled widely and died in a shipwreck off Fire Island on her way back from Italy.

Irmgard Muehlberg

The character of Irmgard Muehlberg owes something to Fredrika Bremer (1801-1865) a Swedish writer and activist who traveled extensively in the United States to study the effect of democratic institutions on society. She visited mills in New England, plantations in the South, and Quaker communities in the mid-Atlantic.

Robert Owen (1771-1858)

Owen was a Welsh textile manufacturer and social reformer. He is known for improving factory working conditions for his workers at New Lanark, a textile mill on the River Clyde in Scotland. In 1824, Owen traveled to America to set up an experimental socialist community at New Harmony, Indiana. It lasted about two years, then Owen returned to England and continued to champion the working class, child labor laws, and free co-educational schools.

Jean Marc Gaspard Itard (1774-1838)

Itard was a French physician and educator of the deaf. He applied his educational theories to the case of Victor of Aveyron. Victor, a feral boy of about twelve, was found wandering naked in the woods of Aveyron in the south of France. Itard took him into his home and tried to civilize/educate him. The 1970 Francois Truffaut film, *The Wild Child*, tells the story.

Edouard Seguin (1812-1880) was Itard's pupil. Seguin dedicated himself to the training of individuals with intellectual disabilities. Following the European revolutions of 1848, Seguin emigrated to the United States where he established a number of special schools, including one in New York City.

The Victorian Orchid Hunters

Orchid hunting became a mania in Britain during the nineteenth century. Orchid hunters braved wild animals, hostile natives, and tropical diseases in their search for the rarest blooms. Valuable plants could change hands for as much as $1,000, about $24,390 in today's money. Most of the profit was made by orchid dealers who financed the trips of the intrepid plant hunters.

PLACES

Benderville

Anyone who has wandered in the Pines has probably come across the ruins of the town and mill at Harrisville on the shores of Harrisville Lake. There had been a bog iron forge on the site, then a paper manufacturing operation called McCartyville, which was taken over by the Harris brothers in 1851. Although Harrisville manufactured paper, not textiles, there was a textile mill in roughly the same period at Sweetwater.

Woodland Place

In the late 19th century, an Italian diplomat/prince married a girl whose family-owned large tracts of land in the Pine Barrens near Chatsworth, then called Shamong. Prince Mario Ruspoli, an attaché at the Italian Embassy in Washington married Pauline de Talleyrand-Perigord, granddaughter of Joseph D. Beers, a New York realty tycoon who had acquired some 25,000 acres in the Pine Barrens. The couple fell in love with the Pines and built a villa on Chatsworth Lake, naming it Chatsworth after the English country seat of the Duke of Devonshire. The name of the town subsequently changed from Shamong to Chatsworth, as it is known today. The prince, with the help of a wealthy Philadelphian, built a lavish country club frequented by Astors, Vanderbilts, and other business and political figures. The Depression put an end to the Chatsworth Club, the prince moved to Belgium, and nothing now remains of house or club.

The North American Phalanx (1843-1858)

The North American Phalanx was a utopian community in Red Bank, New Jersey, based on the principles of the French philosopher, Charles Fourier. In the 1840s, a number of Fourierist communities were established in America. Although the North American Phalanx lasted longer, Brook Farm in Massachusetts (1841-1847) is the most famous thanks to its association with writers and thinkers like Nathaniel Hawthorne, Ralph Waldo Emerson, Bronson Alcott, and Margaret Fuller.

Lowell and Franklinville, Massachusetts

In the early to mid-19th century, Lowell Massachusetts was a manufacturing showplace. In the Lowell System, a model developed by Francis Cabot Lowell, all the processes of textile production were mechanized and located under one roof. To provide labor, Lowell recruited farm girls from the surrounding New England states. The Lowell girls became internationally renowned for their strong work ethic and devotion to self-improvement, attending lectures and classes in the few hours they had between work and sleep. Lowell was visited by writers and reformers like Charles Dickens, Fredrika Bremer, and Ralph Waldo Emerson. There were also many similar, smaller mill towns in Massachusetts. Franklinville is based on one of them, Clinton, Massachusetts, set high above the Nashua River.

About the Author

Perdita Buchan was born in England and came to America as a child. She grew up in Philadelphia and has since lived and worked in New York, London, and Florence, Italy. After many years in Vermont and Massachusetts, she now lives in Ocean Grove, New Jersey.

Perdita Buchan is the author of three previous novels, including *Called Away*, and *The Carousel Carver*, winner of a 2020 Independent Publisher National Book Awards, Mid-Atlantic (Best Regional Fiction). Her nonfiction book, *Utopia, New Jersey: Travels in the Nearest Eden*, was a 2008 NJCH Honor Book. Her short stories and essays have appeared in *The New Yorker*, *Ladies' Home Journal*, *Fiction Network*, *House Beautiful*, *The New York Times*, and *The Christian Science Monitor*, among other publications.

She can be reached through her webpage at www.perditabuchan.com.

Acknowledgements

For their good counsel I would like to thank Linda Howe, Laurel Davis Huber, Mary Walton and Jennifer Caven.